MILLS

Centenary Collection

**Celebrating 100 years of romance with
the very best of Mills & Boon**

*First published in Great Britain 2008
by Harlequin Mills & Boon Limited,
Eton House, 18-24 Paradise Road, Richmond, Surrey TW9 1SR*

© Lucy Gordon 2002

ISBN: 978 0 263 86637 7

77-0208

*Harlequin Mills & Boon policy is to use papers that are
natural, renewable and recyclable products and made from
wood grown in sustainable forests. The logging and
manufacturing processes conform to the legal environmental
regulations of the country of origin.*

*Printed and bound in Spain
by Litografia Rosés S.A., Barcelona*

The King's Bride

by
Lucy Gordon

MILLS & BOON
Pure reading pleasure

Lucy Gordon cut her writing teeth on magazine journalism, interviewing many of the world's most interesting men, including Warren Beatty, Richard Chamberlain, Sir Roger Moore, Sir Alec Guinness, and Sir John Gielgud. She also camped out with lions in Africa and had many other unusual experiences which have often provided the background for her books. She is married to a Venetian, whom she met while on holiday in Venice. They got engaged within two days.

You can visit her website at www.lucy-gordon. com and look out for *The Italian's Passionate Revenge* which will be available in May!

CHAPTER ONE

A SILENCE fell over the packed room. Lizzie looked up quickly, eager to see the man she'd come to find.

His Majesty King Daniel, hereditary ruler of Voltavia, twenty-fifth of his line, thirty-five years old, monarch of his country for the last six months.

Since he'd arrived for his state visit London had been full of official pictures, so she'd thought she knew what he looked like. But while photographs had shown the proud carriage of his head and the stern authority of his lean face, there was no way they could convey the vividness of his features. Lizzie noticed his eyes in particular. They were dark, but with a brilliance that she'd seen only once before, in a picture of his grandfather.

He was tall but carried himself stiffly, and she guessed that a press conference, such as this, came hard to him. In Voltavia he was a monarch, with a good deal of power. He wouldn't take kindly to answering questions from journalists, and Lizzie knew he'd been persuaded to give this conference only for the sake of 'good international relations'.

Before his entrance they had all been warned—no personal questions, no reference to his late wife. No questions about his three children, none of whom had accompanied him to London.

Now he was here and every line of his body showed how ill at ease he felt. He took his seat behind a table on a platform, facing the crowd with a practised air of polite interest.

The questions flowed. They were largely routine and his answers were the same, giving nothing away—the friendship of their two countries—mutual interests, etc, etc. Somebody mentioned his grandfather, the late King Alphonse, whose death, six months earlier, had brought Daniel to the throne. Daniel made a short, restrained speech in praise of his grandfather, whose lasting legacy etc, etc.

In fact, as everyone knew, for the last ten years of his life Alphonse had lived in a twilight world, struck down by a massive stroke. At twenty-five Daniel had become regent, and king in all but name. But Alphonse was still associated with the great days of monarchy. His long reign had begun when kings had had real power, and his personal prestige had ensured that some of it clung to the throne, even as he lay dying.

As Daniel mouthed polite nothings Lizzie mentally compared his features with those of Alphonse, whose personally signed photograph hung on her wall at home. There was a close family resemblance, not only in the dominant nose and firm chin, but in the expression of the face: proud, closed, unyielding.

They'd said of Alphonse that he was the handsomest man of his generation, and had still been saying it when he was in his eighties. But they'd said, too, that he was the most puritanical. He could have had any number of liaisons, but he'd been a faithful husband for twenty years. After his wife had died, if he'd indulged himself he'd been so discreet that the world had never been quite sure.

Only one woman had aroused him to a public display of admiration, and that was the great musical comedy star, Lizzie Boothe. She'd visited Voltavia with her own company, and the King had attended her performances. Perhaps she'd also given performances in private. Nobody knew for certain, and the King's reputation for rigid respectability remained untouched.

Daniel was the image of his splendid grandfather in looks, and also in the pattern of his life. Married young to a suitable princess, he had been a devoted husband and father, and had led a discreet life since his wife's death, three years earlier.

At last the questions were over and everybody stood in line so that the King could meet them individually. Down the line he came, stopping for a few moments with each person, shaking hands, asking banal questions about things he couldn't possibly care about, and receiving banal answers with the appearance of polite interest. He must be bored out of his skull, Lizzie thought, but he kept going resolutely.

At last he reached her and stood, professional smile in place, while his aide announced, 'Miss Elizabeth Boothe.'

His pause was only a fraction of a second, his smile never wavered. But she was close enough to see his eyes and the slight shock in them. So the name was still remembered in Voltavia. That pleased her.

As he shook her hand the King glanced at the identity tag on her shoulder, bearing only her name. 'The others list also their publications,' he observed. 'I think you are not a journalist.'

'That's true, Your Majesty,' Lizzie said, smiling.

He did not release her hand. 'You are, perhaps, an actress?'

Any man, looking at her flamboyant beauty and glorious mane of red hair might be forgiven for thinking so.

'I'm not an actress,' she said, 'but my great-aunt was. She was called Lizzie Boothe, and had many admirers in your country.'

Again the slight shock in his eyes: surprise, she thought, that she'd dared to mention such a delicate subject.

'Indeed,' he said in a neutral voice, and prepared to pass on, but Lizzie spoke hurriedly. 'I'm a historian, Your Majesty. I'm writing a book about King Alphonse, and I hoped you would grant me an interview.'

She'd tightened her hand on his, detaining him against his will, an outrageous breach of protocol as his astonished look told her. Instead of backing off she held him a little longer, meeting his eyes. It was a risk, but she'd never been afraid of that. At his side his aide tensed, ready to force her to release him at a signal from him. But it didn't come, and gradually the amazement in his eyes gave way to something else. Interest? Curiosity? Lizzie's heart beat with excitement. She was almost there...

Then blankness came down over his eyes like a curtain, and he pulled his hand out of hers. 'You must forgive me,' he said stiffly. 'I do not give private interviews.'

A curt nod of his head, and he passed on.

It was over. They were all being shepherded out, politely but firmly. Annoyed with herself, Lizzie returned to the neat little London house she'd inherited five years ago from her actress great-aunt, Dame Elizabeth Boothe, as she'd been at the end of her life. The Dame, as everyone had called her, had lived surrounded by mementoes of her great days: gifts from admirers, theatre programmes, some of them fifty years old, and pictures of herself in glory.

Lizzie had loved the Dame. Now she kept the house much as it had been when she'd inherited it.

On one wall was a huge coloured photograph of the actress at the height of her beauty and fame. Next to it was a picture of her most notable admirer, King Alphonse, taken when he was nearly seventy, imposing, autocratic, but still astonishingly good-looking. Near the bottom was written, in the King's own hand, *In friendship and gratitude, Alphonse*.

Lizzie tossed her bag onto a chair and confronted Dame Elizabeth.

'I made a mess of it,' she told her. 'Nothing happened the way I meant it to, and I just antagonised him. You'd think I'd know better, wouldn't you? I am supposed to be a professional.'

The Dame's eyes were laughing, her head thrown back in an ecstasy of song, but Lizzie could read her thoughts.

'I know, I know! Dress the part. That's what you used to say. And I didn't. If I'd worn tweeds and horn-rimmed spectacles I suppose he'd have taken me seriously. But why shouldn't I dress as I like?'

Good question! If a historian was a modern young woman, five feet ten with ravishing red hair and a model figure, why shouldn't she wear skirts short enough to show off her silken legs, and suicidally high heels? Why shouldn't she make up to emphasise her large green eyes and wide mouth that seemed made for the pleasures of life, of which laughter was only one?

If there was an answer, it was because she was as serious

about her work as her appearance, which was very serious indeed. And today she'd blown it.

'There was one moment when I thought I was winning,' she told the picture. 'He looked at me in such way that I thought—I was almost sure—but he just got away from me at the last minute. *You* wouldn't have let him get away, would you?' She sighed. 'And I won't get a second chance, either.'

But, against the odds, the second chance presented itself next morning in the shape of a gilt-edged card announcing that King Daniel was pleased to invite her to a ball at the Voltavian embassy that very evening. After a whoop of triumph she got down to the deadly earnest business of making an impact.

The evening dress she chose was black velvet and swept the floor, but there all semblance of decorum ended. It was cut to show off her shoulders and bosom. The neckline was within the bounds of propriety, but only just. The bodice clung, and fitted tightly all the way down to her small waist, before outlining the flare of her hips, the length of her thighs and then down to her ankles. It would have been impossible to walk in such a dress but for the slit at the rear, through which the vision of her stunning legs came and went.

It was a dress for a woman who wanted to be noticed and could *afford* to be noticed: not always the same thing, as the Dame had frequently observed in her most caustic voice.

Lizzie had booked the cab with time to spare. No matter what the function, the rule was that royalty arrived last. To be late was to be shut out.

To her relief she reached the embassy in good time, and was shown into the great ballroom that looked as though time had passed it by. Glittering chandeliers hung overhead, the mirrors were framed by gilt, and its glamour was the glamour of another age. At the far end was a dais with a throne. Over it hung the coat of arms of Voltavia, dominated by a snarling bear. For a thousand years the bear had been the country's symbol.

When every guest was in place, fanning themselves and desperate for a drink, the great doors at one end of the room swung open, and the King began the long walk to the throne at the far end.

Lizzie recalled the Dame describing a ball at the palace in Voltavia, with King Alphonse in full dress military uniform, glittering with gold braid. 'So splendid, my dear! So magnificent!' Kings didn't dress like that any more, which Lizzie thought a pity, but she ceased to regret it when she saw Daniel in white tie and tails, which seemed to emphasise his height and the breadth of his shoulders. On some men, anything was magnificent.

First there were the duty dances. The King took the floor with a succession of titled ladies—a member of the British royal family, the ambassador's wife, the wife of a prominent international banker. Lizzie guessed there were a lot to go before he reached her.

She wasn't short of partners, and Frederick, one of the king's aides, solicited her hand several times. He danced well and asked her many questions about herself. Acting on orders, she thought, and kept her answers light and unrevealing. If Daniel wanted to know about her, he could do his own asking.

Occasionally the dance brought them close, but he never looked in her direction. That might have been courtesy to his partner, but once, when he wasn't dancing, Lizzie glanced up to where he sat alone on the throne and found him watching her. After that she knew he was conscious of her even when he wasn't looking.

At last Frederick approached her again, not to dance this time but to give a correct little bow and ask, 'Would you like the honour of dancing with His Majesty?'

'Thank you. I would.'

She followed him to Daniel, who watched her approach. She sank into a curtsey, but unlike the other women, who lowered their heads, Lizzie curtseyed with her head up, eyes meeting his in direct challenge. He nodded slightly in her direction, before extending his arm. She took it and he led her onto the floor for the waltz.

He was a good dancer, every step correct, but his body was tense. By contrast, Lizzie danced like liquid, gliding this way and that in his arms.

'I'm glad you were able to accept at such short notice,' he said.

Lizzie made the appropriate speech about being honoured before saying, 'I wonder how Your Majesty knew where to send the invitation.'

'I had you investigated,' he informed her calmly, 'and discovered you to be a historian, as you said. I gather you've written many letters to the Information Office in Voltavia.'

'Yes, and I've got nowhere. They just brush me off. But I *am* serious.'

'So I understand. The list of your degrees and professorships is impressive—and alarming.'

'There's no need for Your Majesty to be alarmed,' she said demurely. 'I don't bite.'

'But you do pursue. When you contrived to get yourself a

place at the press reception—oh, yes, I know that too—you were in pursuit, were you not?'

'That's right.'

'And I was the prey?'

'Naturally. I only pursue the big bears. They're the most rewarding.'

He looked down at her with a faint, curious smile. 'And do you think you'll find me "rewarding"?'

'I'm not sure yet. It depends whether you give me what I want.'

'And is that how you judge men—by whether they give you what you want?'

Lizzie raised delicate eyebrows in well simulated surprise. 'But of course. What other yardstick is there?'

'Are you by any chance trying to flirt with me, Miss Boothe?'

'Certainly not,' she said, shocked. 'It would be improper for any woman to flirt with the King.'

'True.'

'It's for the King to flirt with her.'

Her demure tone took him off guard, and he frowned, as though unsure that he'd heard her correctly. Then he smiled, cautiously.

'And if the King didn't flirt with her?' he asked. 'Might she not show a little enterprise in the matter?'

'She wouldn't dare,' Lizzie informed him, straight-faced. 'Lest he think her impertinent.'

'I don't think you fear the opinion of any man, Miss Boothe.'

'But Your Majesty is a king, not a man.'

'Is that what you think?'

She looked straight into his face, saying demurely, 'I'm waiting for you to tell me what to think.'

'By heaven, you're a cool one!' he exclaimed softly.

'But of course. A woman would need to stay cool when entering the bear's cave,' she pointed out. 'Unless she's well protected.'

'You, I think, are protected by your effrontery.'

'Oh, dear! I have offended Your Majesty.'

His eyes gleamed. 'Do not fish for compliments, Miss Boothe.'

'Is that what I was doing?' she murmured.

'Yes. And it was quite unnecessary.'

There were a dozen ways to take that but, raising a questioning eyebrow to him, she sensed exactly what he was telling her and a swift excitement scurried through her veins.

She hadn't meant this to happen. So far and no further. That had been the idea. Flirt with him, intrigue him until he was putty in her hands. It had worked before.

'Use your charms to bring them to heel,' Dame Elizabeth had always advised. 'What else are charms *for*?'

But it had never been part of the plan for *him* to charm *her*. Now matters were getting out of hand. Beneath his stiff exterior this man had a devil in his eyes. Lizzie had an uneasy feeling that he'd sized her up and decided he could deal with her.

But how? That was the question that made her blood race. Whatever the answer she decided she was going to enjoy it, and if she could gain her professional goals as well, so much the better.

'The music is ending,' Daniel observed. 'But our talk is just beginning. I've ordered champagne served on the terrace.'

Two hundred pairs of eyes watched him lead her from the floor and through the French windows that led onto the broad terrace. A footman was just laying down a tray bearing two fluted glasses and a bottle. Daniel waved him away, indicated for Lizzie to sit at the small table, and himself did the pouring.

'So you're writing a book about my grandfather?' he said, putting the glass into her hand and seating himself opposite. Through the tall windows Lizzie could see couples swirling by as the dance resumed, and hear the soft swell of music. But she was intensely conscious of the King, watching her closely, as though she was the only person in the world. 'Why do you wish to do this?'

'Because he's fascinated me all my life,' she replied. 'Aunt Lizzie told me so much about him, and about Voltavia. She made it sound like a wonderful country.'

'It *is* a wonderful country. And I know she had many admirers there. Among whom, of course, was the King.'

'She always kept the medals and decorations he gave her. She was a compulsive hoarder. I don't think she ever threw anything away. When she died she left everything to me, and I still have them all—the medals, the scrapbooks, even some of her costumes.'

'You must have meant a great deal to her.'

'She was my grandfather's sister and almost the only family I had. When I was ten my parents died and she took me in. She was thought very scandalous when she was young, but when I knew her she'd become Dame Elizabeth Boothe, and very respectable.'

'And I suppose you were completely in her confidence?'

Lizzie considered. 'Not completely. I don't think she told

everything to anyone. She lived in the public eye but she kept many secrets.'

'But some secrets are harder to keep than others.'

'If you mean the fact that King Alphonse admired her, no, that was hardly a secret, especially with all the jewellery he gave her.'

'He gave her jewels? I must admit I didn't know that.'

Lizzie touched the diamond necklace and matching earrings that blazed against her fair skin. 'These came from him.'

Daniel looked hard at the flashing gems. 'Magnificent,' he murmured. 'Clearly he valued her a great deal. But how did she value him?'

'She kept his photograph on her wall to the end of her life.' Daniel shrugged, and she said quickly, 'No, it wasn't just a formal picture. It was inscribed in his own handwriting.'

He was suddenly alert. 'What did he write?'

'"In friendship and gratitude, Alphonse,"' Lizzie replied.

'"Friendship and gratitude,"' Daniel repeated slowly. 'Yes, my grandfather was a restrained man. I can imagine him using such words when what he really meant was something else—something a great deal more intense and emotional.'

There was a new note in his voice as he said the last words that made the silence hang heavy between them. For a mad moment Lizzie wondered if she'd strayed into something that was too much for her. This man held every card in the pack, yet she was trying to gamble with him on equal terms. It was heady wine, and his sudden urgent tone made it headier still.

The music of the waltz was floating out onto the terrace.

'Dance with me,' he commanded, taking her into his arms without waiting for her answer.

In the ballroom he had danced correctly, preserving the proper distance of a few inches between them, and touching her back so lightly that she'd barely felt it. Now he held her close enough for her to feel his breath on her bare shoulder, and his hand was firm in the small of her back. She had said that he was only a king, not a man. And she'd been so wrong.

'What do they call you?' he murmured. 'Liz? Elizabeth?'

'Lizzie.'

'Lizzie, I'm glad we've had this talk. It makes many things clearer.'

'Do you mean that you'll help me?' she asked eagerly.

'Ah, yes, you want an interview.'

'And much, much more.'

There was a sudden keen look in his eyes. 'How much more?' he asked.

'Access to the royal archives,' she said, breathless with hope. 'Official memos, private correspondence…'

'*Private—?*' With a swift movement his hand tightened on her waist, drawing her hard against him.

'I want to show him in the round, and for that I must see everything,' she said, speaking breathlessly for he was holding her very tightly. 'We all know the face he presented to the world, but it's the things the world didn't know that have real value.'

'Ah, yes. Value. We mustn't forget that. And of course their value is higher precisely *because* the world doesn't know.'

'Exactly. There's no substitute for private letters.'

'I'm sure that's true,' he murmured, sending warm breath skittering across her cheek. She saw how very close his mouth was to her own, and tried to control her riotous thoughts. But they wouldn't be controlled. They raced ahead, speculating about the shape of his mouth, the firmness of his lips, how they would feel against hers...

She looked up and what she saw gave her a shock. Despite the apparent ardour in his behaviour there was only cool calculation in his eyes.

She tried to clear her head, to know what this meant, but that was hard when the world was spinning around her. As they slowed she realised that he had danced her right around the corner of the building. He was smiling at her, and she could believe, if she wanted to, that the chill look of a moment ago had been all her imagination.

'You're not the only historian who wants to write about my grandfather, Miss Boothe.'

'No, but I'm ahead of the pack,' she said simply.

'Are you?'

'Yes. Because of Aunt Lizzie, who knew him as nobody else did.'

'I wasn't forgetting that, nor that such knowledge is *valuable*.' He stressed the word in a way that fell oddly on her ear.

'Priceless,' she agreed.

'I'd hardly say priceless. Sooner or later most things have a price. The problem is agreeing on it.'

'I'm not sure that I understand Your Majesty.'

He smiled. 'I think you do. I think we understand each other very well, and have done from the beginning.'

The reserve had gone from his eyes, replaced by something that made her heart beat faster. Almost unconsciously she raised her face towards him as he lowered his mouth onto hers.

She was no green girl experiencing her first kiss, but it might almost have been the first from its effect on her. There'd been a time when a king had held his throne by being better, stronger, more skilled at everything than his subjects, and perhaps it was still partly true, for this king kissed like an expert, ardent, subtle, knowing how to seek out a woman's weakness. Lizzie had never been kissed like this before, not even by the eager young husband with whom she'd shared a few months of wild passion before parting in bitterness.

His mouth caressed hers with urgency. In repose his lips were firm almost to the point of hardness, but now their movements were teasing, driving her as though he was being harried by his own desire. She tried to master her own rising excitement, determined to stay in control, but he was equally determined to strip control away from her. And he was winning.

He kissed the soft skin beneath one ear and she gave a small gasp. She was so sensitive there that normally she tried never to let a man approach it, but he'd known her weakness by instinct and gone for it without mercy. He continued the subtle assault down her long neck while she trembled and clung to him.

When he raised his head she longed to pull it down to her again and tell him to continue what he'd begun. Instead she became hypnotised by his eyes, which were brooding over her as though he too was trying to comprehend her, and failing.

'You came here tonight for a purpose,' he murmured. 'Was this it?'

'I—don't know,' she said wildly. 'Perhaps—'

'Ah, yes, the letters. Words on paper between people who are dead and gone. But we are alive. No woman ever felt so alive in my arms as you.'

And no man had ever made her feel so vibrant with life. Her head was swimming.

A noise from nearby made him release her reluctantly.

'We must talk more—in Voltavia,' he said. 'I leave tomorrow. You will follow me next week.'

It was more than she'd hoped for but she couldn't help rebelling against this diktat. She wasn't one of his subjects.

'Will I indeed?' she asked.

'If you're serious about what you're after, yes. Be there on Wednesday. If not—'

'I'll be there,' she said quickly, fearful of seeing the prize snatched away. 'I promise.'

'Of course,' he said, amused. 'There was never any question of your refusing. No, don't be angry with me. I hold all the cards, and you know it.'

It would have been wonderful to take him down a peg, but she was too close to her dream to risk it. She took the arm he proffered and they walked sedately back along the terrace to the little table. Frederick was waiting for them, with the reminder of an ambassador's wife who must be honoured. Daniel inclined his head graciously to Lizzie.

'I shall be waiting,' he said softly. 'Don't disappoint me.'

He walked away, leaving her to return to the ballroom on Frederick's arm. She felt as though she was walking on air. The glittering professional prize had been held out to her. That, she told herself, was the reason for the swift beating of her heart. That, and no other reason.

But she was deceiving herself, and she knew it.

* * *

When the last guest had departed the King relaxed with a brandy and soda, indicating for Frederick, his most trusted aide, to join him.

'Did she say anything of importance to you?' Daniel asked.

'Not a thing, sir. She replied to all my questions but revealed nothing at all.'

'That's no more than I expected. This is an extremely clever lady, but I have her measure.' A wry smile broke over Daniel's face. 'She's going to be a pleasure to do battle with. You know the plan?'

'Yes, sir.' Frederick took a deep breath before venturing to say, 'You don't think that this way of doing things is a little—a little…?' His voice ran down as his nerve ran out.

Daniel took pity on him. 'Devious, unprincipled, cold-blooded?'

Frederick ran a finger around his collar. 'Those are Your Majesty's words.'

'Coward,' Daniel said without rancour. 'Yes, Frederick, I'm being all those things. But then, so is she. This is no ordinary lady. She's sharp, shrewd, and utterly unscrupulous. So the only way I can fight her is to be the same.'

CHAPTER TWO

'A WOMAN is never too old to be glamorous,' the Dame had been fond of declaring to her awe-struck young relative, and she had lived up to her philosophy to the end. Life with the great lady had been fun because she'd never been less than exotic.

But it was Bess who'd mothered the teenage Lizzie. Bess had been Dame Elizabeth's dresser when she trod the boards, and in old age she'd still been her all-purpose maid and companion. When Lizzie had returned from boarding school it had been Bess who'd made sure she was comfortable, checked what she liked to eat, put flowers in her room. When Lizzie had gone out on a date it had been Elizabeth who'd lectured her about 'man management', which had been fun, even though the advice was often out of date. But it was Bess who'd waited up to make sure she was home safely, and Bess in whom she'd confided.

One time the Dame's advice had been spot-on when she'd tried to warn Lizzie off Toby Wrenworth, a dare-devil motorbike rider.

'That young man was made to be a lover, not a husband,' she'd declared in her booming voice. 'Don't confuse the two.'

'Auntie!' Lizzie had exclaimed, not sure whether to be amused or aghast. 'You're not actually advising me to—?'

'I'm advising you not to confuse the two,' the Dame had repeated firmly.

But the eighteen-year-old Lizzie had ignored the advice, and in due course she'd wished she'd heeded it. The Dame had glared all through their wedding, but when the inevitable divorce happened, two years later, she'd been a rock. If she hadn't over-flowed with sympathy neither had she uttered reproaches.

'Stop crying and get yourself off to college,' she'd commanded. 'It's what you should have done before, instead of wasting time on a man who was all teeth and trousers.'

The robust approach had done Lizzie a world of good. For sympathy she'd turned to Bess, and they'd cried together.

Even as a teenager she'd been sensitive enough to feel sad for the maid who lived in her employer's shadow and had no life of her own, although she'd always seemed contented enough with her lot. Since the great lady's death Bess had lived in a re-tirement home. It was a comfortable, even luxurious place, with large gardens filled with flowers, and Bess seemed happy there.

Lizzie visited whenever she could, and made a point of going to see her friend before she left for Voltavia. Bess was old and frail, but her mind was clear, and her first words were eager. 'Tell me all about your lovers.'

'Lovers? Plural? You think I'm living a really exotic life, don't you?'

'I think you're a pretty girl, and a pretty girl should have lovers.'

'Well, I have a boyfriend or two.'

'Do they break your heart?'

'Do you *want* them to?' Lizzie asked with a chuckle.

'No, of course not. But I worry that it isn't possible. You've been rather *armoured* since Toby.'

'Good thing too.'

'No, my dear. A woman should stay open to love, no matter how much it hurts.'

'But I am. You should have seen me at the embassy ball. Flirting. And more.'

'That's different, and you know it. Throwing out lures, as we used to say, because you're hoping to catch a prize.'

'Yes, and I caught him too. Oh, Bess, he's eating out of my hand. I'm that close to those archives.'

'Yes, dear, but you're hiding—as always. Work is such a convenient excuse, isn't it?'

Bess's eyes saw too much, Lizzie thought. Abruptly she changed the subject.

'What I came to tell you is that I'm off to Voltavia tomorrow.'

Bess's old eyes sparkled. 'How lucky you are!' she exclaimed softly. 'It's such a wonderful country.'

'Of course, you went there with Auntie, didn't you?'

'That's right. If only you could have seen her. She was at the height of her beauty, and she made a kind of triumphal procession around the main cities, and then she performed for the court. She was guest of honour at a ball, and danced with the King.'

'Did you see him, Bess?'

'Oh, yes. I was there too, in a little ante-room, so that I could look after her when she needed to take the weight off her feet. What's King Daniel like? I've seen his pictures, but they make him look rather cold.'

'He does, just at first. But there's something about him that isn't cold at all. I'm sure of it.'

Bess nodded, smiling. 'Ah, yes. Something deep inside, and he won't let you reach it until he's ready. Just like his grandfather.'

'Did the Dame tell you that?' Lizzie asked with a chuckle.

For answer Bess laid a finger over her lips, with a look of mischief.

'Have a wonderful trip, Lizzie, dear. And come and see me when you get back.'

Voltavia lay in the very centre of Europe, with borders that touched France, Switzerland and Germany. It had a population of a million, four cities, one important river, three official languages—English, French and German—and one airport.

Lizzie emerged from Arrivals to be greeted by a driver in the palace uniform. He took charge of her bags and escorted her to a waiting limousine. When she was settled in the back he showed her the well-stocked bar, asked what she would like to drink, and poured her an orange juice.

'It's thirty miles to the palace,' he said, taking his place behind the wheel. 'I hope you enjoy the journey.'

The first part of the trip lay through some of the most magnificent rugged scenery Lizzie had ever seen. She watched, holding her breath, as mountains gave way to pine forests, where wild bears still roamed, and then to lakes, serene and impossibly blue under the summer sky. At last they neared Durmann, the capital, turning off just before the city to sweep down the long approach to the palace.

It was a grand structure, a quarter mile long and built from a honey-coloured stone that looked beautiful in the soft glow of the sunset. Two Z-shaped staircases adorned the front, on one of which a man was waiting to greet her. Lizzie recognised Frederick from the ball. Smiling, he explained that he would be her host until the King was free.

They embarked on what seemed like a long journey, down endless corridors, until at last they reached the apartment set aside for her use. It was a charming place, a bedroom, a living room and bathroom, with modern facilities, yet a touch of old-worlde grandeur. When Frederick had gone Lizzie stripped off for a shower and a change of clothes that left her feeling ready to tackle anything, even Daniel.

Especially Daniel. Wryly she made the admission to herself.

She wasn't only here as a historian seeking facts. She was here as a woman who'd been passionately kissed and wasn't prepared to let it go at that. She considered the elegant trouser suit she'd just put on, and was dissatisfied with it. The green silk dress would be better. It took a moment to change and brush out her red hair again. Dame Elizabeth would have been proud of her.

And so, perhaps, would Bess. 'Be open to love,' she'd said, and the soft pounding of Lizzie's heart was warning her that suddenly she wasn't as armoured as usual.

The knock on the door brought a smile to her lips. Daniel at last.

But it wasn't Daniel.

'Your supper,' Frederick said, ushering in a footman with a trolley.

Supper was delicious, a wide selection of dishes, all perfectly prepared, and a bottle of excellent wine. Frederick was charming company, but he wasn't Daniel.

'I expect you want to go to bed now,' he said at last, rising. 'I'm sorry His Majesty couldn't see you today, but I'm sure it'll be early tomorrow.'

They bade each other a civil goodnight and he departed, leaving Lizzie feeling very cross indeed. She reminded herself that Daniel hadn't specified a time. She couldn't really complain. It was just…

She sighed. It was just that if he'd been half as eager to see her as she was to see him he would have rushed to her.

She watched satellite television for an hour, but took nothing in. She went to stand on her balcony overlooking the front of the palace, where floodlights picked out the two staircases and highlighted the building's elegant, symmetrical beauty. From somewhere above her head a clock chimed midnight. She returned indoors and closed the windows.

He wasn't coming now. She took another shower and put on a soft peach silk nightdress before climbing into the vast antique bed that looked big enough for ten. It had probably been built for an orgy, she thought despondently. It certainly hadn't been intended for a solitary sleeper.

She wasn't sure when she fell asleep, or how much time passed, but it was very dark when she opened her eyes to the sound of somebody knocking on the outer door of her apartment. She whisked on the peach silk robe that matched her nightdress and hurried out of the bedroom to the main room. The soft tap on her front door came again, and she opened it cautiously.

The corridor outside was dimly lit, and empty except for one man.

'Good evening,' Daniel said with a smile. 'Forgive me for arriving at such an untimely hour, but I thought it best to be discreet.'

'Of course,' she agreed, backing away to let him in.

Daniel quietly closed the door behind him. Lizzie went

to the main light switch, but he halted her with his hand
on her wrist.

'I think not,' he said, switching on a very small table lamp.
'This will be sufficient.'

The tiny lamp gave a reasonable illumination, while still
leaving the room half hidden in shadow. But she could discern
enough of Daniel to feast her eyes. He was in day clothes,
but without a jacket, his shirt open at the throat, looking more
informal than she'd seen him before.

Lizzie felt at a slight disadvantage. She was sufficiently
worldly wise to have realised that this moment would probably
come. Even to hope for it. But had she hoped for it quite so soon?

Then she put her chin up. She was alone with the most dan-
gerously attractive man she'd ever met, his dark eyes were
regarding her with appreciation, and if she couldn't cope
with that then it was time she retired from the fray and took
up something easier, like taming lions.

'I'm sure you understand why I've come here so late, and
so discretely,' he said, still with his eyes on her. 'In fact, I've
been sure that we shared a perfect understanding from the
first moment. Neither of us is exactly inexperienced in the
ways of—shall we say—intrigue?'

She smiled, beginning to feel at ease. 'Does it matter what
we call it?'

'Some people believe that to define things exactly is es-
sential. Others feel that if the essence is right, the rest is
froth. You clearly belong in the second group, which I must
admit surprises me a little.'

'Oh? Why?'

'As a historian I should have thought you valued precise
definition. And you are here as a historian, are you not?'

'In the presence of a king I am always a historian,' she riposted. 'Among other things.'

He laughed. 'Yes, let us not forget that I'm a king, because if I weren't you wouldn't be here.'

Not strictly true, she thought, looking at his throat and the few inches of chest she could see beneath it, rising and falling with some emotion that excited her. There was more excitement when he touched her face and wreathed his fingers in the hair that fell over her shoulders, drawing her swiftly close to cradle her head against his shoulder.

He covered her mouth swiftly and suddenly, kissing her with lips that demanded more than caressed. There was no tenderness, just an assertion of power, but while one part of her rebelled at this, another part, infuriatingly, was thrilled at the complete, unquestioning confidence of this man. His power came less from his rank than from his ability to drive a woman into a turmoil of dizzying sensation by his kiss alone. When he released her she was gasping, and shocked at how easily he could make her want to yield.

His face bore a look of resolution, as though he'd just come to a decision. Lizzie waited with pounding heart for what he would say next. But when the words came, they were the last she had expected.

'I think the time has come to drop all pretence between us,' he said in a voice that was curiously hard for a man in the throes of passion.

'I'm not sure I understand you.'

'I believe you do. When we spoke in London I had—shall we say certain suspicions? Which you obligingly confirmed. You've come here to sell, and I am prepared to buy.'

'Prepared—to buy?' Lizzie echoed slowly, trying to silence the monstrous thought that had reared up in her brain.

'At a sensible price, yes. You obviously know the value of what you bring to market—'

'And what *exactly* is it that you think I bring to market?' Lizzie asked, her eyes narrowing.

He looked surprised for a moment, but then shrugged. 'You're quite right to put negotiations on a businesslike footing. I'm prepared to be reasonable about money, even generous, but don't try to overcharge me—'

He got no further. What he might have said next was cut off by a stinging slap from a very angry woman. Then they were staring at each other, each trying to believe that it had happened.

Lizzie had never slapped a man's face before. She considered it undignified and violent. Now, in a turmoil of hurt pride, hurt feelings and sheer outrage, she was discovering how satisfying it could be.

'Have you any idea,' he said slowly, 'of the penalty for attacking the King?'

'Don't make me laugh!' she stormed, in the worst temper of her life. 'All right, go on. Summon the guards and tell them that you tried to buy your way into my bed and got your face slapped. I don't think so. No man has ever had me for money, and no man ever will. King or no king! And if you thought I was for sale when you invited me here, boy, did you make a mistake!'

He was paler than she'd ever seen any man. Doubtless from the shock of being treated so disrespectfully, she thought with grim satisfaction.

'And I,' he said at last, 'have never needed to buy my way into a woman's bed. Nor am I interested in your charms.'

'That's a lie,' she said, casting caution to the winds.

He shrugged. 'Possibly. But I have never allowed my personal desires to interfere with politics, and you would do well to remember that in our dealings.'

'We're not going to have any more dealings,' she said breathlessly.

'That is for *me* to say. When we've discussed business I will inform you of our future dealings.'

'Why, you arrogant—'

'Of course I am. I'm a king; what did you expect?' His eyes gleamed at her. 'We're not just characters in books. There's still a reality behind the title, and the reality is power, especially here and now. I've wasted enough time. I want the letters.'

'Letters? What letters?'

'Oh, please! You know what you're here for.'

'I know what I'm not here for, and if you come any closer—'

His eyes flicked over her without interest. 'You flatter yourself—at least for the moment,' he said coldly. 'All that concerns me is the bundle of letters in your possession.'

'I don't know what you're talking about.'

He sighed. 'Very well, we must play the game out—although I had credited you with more intelligence. When we were in London, you yourself told me of the relationship between your great-aunt and my grandfather.'

'Well yes, except that nobody really knew for certain—'

'*I* know for certain. They were lovers. Their correspondence leaves no doubt of the fact.'

The historian stirred in her. 'Correspondence?'

'When I assumed the throne I went through all my grandfather's possessions. Among them was a locked chest that turned out to contain a pile of letters. They were from an English woman who signed herself "your own Liz, for ever".'

'You mean they were love letters?'

'Yes, they were love letters, and they totally undermine my grandfather's reputation.'

'I don't understand.'

'He was known and respected as a rigid disciplinarian, a stern patriarch and an aloof monarch. Royalty, he believed, should "keep a proper distance". Because he lived up to his beliefs he was deeply respected, all over the world.'

'But he didn't "keep a proper distance" from this lady?'

'It would appear not. The letters are emotional and indiscreet, and they strongly suggest that his replies must have been the same.' Daniel's eyes narrowed. 'But I imagine you could tell me about that?'

'Me? Why should you think I know anything?'

'Because the replies are in your possession. You are Dame Elizabeth's heir, the one she trusted to preserve her legend. Who else?'

'But she never mentioned anything like this. And who's to say it was her? Did this woman ever sign her full name?'

'No, it was always "Liz", but she's the only possibility. The dates are very revealing. In August 1955 she wrote saying how much she had enjoyed seeing him again, and how sad she was to have left him. Dame Elizabeth was touring Voltavia in July 1955, and returned to England in the first week in August.'

'That certainly looks likely. But why did she never tell me?'

'If that's meant to be a negotiating ploy, let me warn you that it isn't a good one.'

'Look, I knew nothing about this.'

'Nonsense! You as good as admitted that you had them when we spoke in London.'

'I—?'

'All that talk about the value of personal letters. You stressed that your great-aunt knew King Alphonse *as nobody else did*, and that such knowledge was priceless. That was your exact word.'

'Yes, but I didn't mean—'

'And I, you may remember, said that sooner or later a price could always be agreed. You have my grandfather's letters and you've kept them to publish. It would be treasure-trove to a historian. But I don't mean to see my family secrets bandied about for the world to laugh at. You will hand them over to me. I'll pay a reasonable price, but I won't be trifled with.'

The truth was dawning on Lizzie. 'Is that the reason you brought me here—the only reason?' she demanded, aghast.

'What other reason could there be?'

She thought of his kiss, how giddy it had made her. And she'd rushed here, dreaming of more sweet delight. She could have screamed with vexation.

Instead she spoke with careful restraint. 'We seem to have misunderstood each other. I don't have your grandfather's letters. I don't even know that they exist. The Dame may have destroyed them. Have you thought of that?'

'Please!' he said dismissively. 'A woman? Destroy love letters? Is any woman discreet enough for that?'

'Is any *man*? Alphonse didn't destroy his, did he? I don't think you should get on your high horse about indiscretion.'

That annoyed him, she was glad to see. He flushed angrily

and snapped, 'This argument gets us nowhere. I *know* you have these letters—'

'Rubbish! You know nothing of the kind!'

'Do not interrupt me. I know you have these letters because you virtually offered them to me in London.'

'I did not. I mentioned personal correspondence because that's what a historian always wants to see. I didn't know what you were reading into it.'

'You went out of your way to assure me that Dame Elizabeth kept *everything*.'

'But I didn't mean this. How could I when I knew nothing about it? If they were in the house I'd have found them.'

'A bank deposit box?'

'She'd have told me.'

They glared at each other in frustration.

'What are they like, these letters you found?' Lizzie asked, trying to sound casual.

'That doesn't concern you.'

'The hell it doesn't! You drag me out here under false pretences and *it doesn't concern me*? You'll find out whether it does or not.'

'If that's a threat, Miss Boothe, let me warn you, *don't*! People don't cross swords with me.'

'Time someone did! Frankly I wish I did have the letters you want, then I could enjoy telling you to whistle for them. As it is, I don't have them, don't know where they are, have never heard of them. Which rather takes the gilt off the gingerbread.'

His eyes were cold and narrow with displeasure, and if Lizzie had been easily afraid she would have started to quake now. But she was naturally impulsive, lost her temper, said too much, regretted it too late, and only realised the danger when it was long past. Daniel would have had to lock her in a dungeon before it dawned on Lizzie that just maybe she'd gone a little bit too far.

Possibly this occurred to him, because he relaxed and allowed his anger to fade into exasperation. 'There's nothing more to be gained tonight,' he growled. 'We'll talk tomorrow afternoon.'

'Unless I decide to leave before then,' she said with spirit.

'Well, if I find you gone I'll know what to think,' he said smoothly. 'Goodnight, Miss Boothe.'

She was facing a closed door.

'Tomorrow afternoon,' she breathed. 'Or tomorrow evening. Or the day after, if it suits you. Oh, no! I don't think so.'

Moving fast, she dressed, hurled some clothes into a bag and headed for the outer door. Opening it slowly, quietly, she prepared to step outside.

But, instead of the empty corridor she'd seen earlier, she now discovered two beefy guards standing across the doorway, firmly blocking her exit.

CHAPTER THREE

IT WAS hard for Lizzie to maintain her indignation when the sun rose on a scene of glorious summer. The beautifully manicured gardens were spread before her, trees, shrubs, flowers, winding paths, and in the distance a gleam of water. She had seldom known such a beautiful day, or such enchanting surroundings.

But she was annoyed. She must remember that.

She showered and changed into a cream linen trouser suit with a sleeveless green sweater. She finished off with a chain about her neck plus matching earrings. She was pleased with the effect. The chain was gold, but the bulky earrings had been bought cheaply from a market stall.

It occurred to her that she was all dressed up with nowhere to go, effectively a prisoner in this apartment until Daniel chose to let her out. But before her temper had a chance to get started there was a knock on the outer door.

'Come in,' she called.

Frederick appeared, leading a footman pushing a trolley on which food was piled.

'No,' Lizzie said firmly. 'I want to see the King, right now.'

'I'm afraid that won't be—' He got no further. Lizzie was out of the door and darting down the corridor.

She ran, expecting every moment to be stopped, but nobody tried. She had a reasonable idea which direction she wanted because Frederick had led her past Daniel's apartments the day before. After taking a couple of wrong turnings she found herself on the right corridor. At the far end was a large pair of oak doors with two guards standing outside. They moved together when they saw her, making it impossible for her to get between them, but she managed to knock loudly.

The door was answered by a man dressed in a neat grey suit. Everything else about him was grey also, including his demeanour.

'I would like to see the King,' Lizzie said as firmly as she could manage.

'Your name, please?'

'Elizabeth Boothe.'

The man looked puzzled. 'But His Majesty is on his way to see you. He left only a moment ago.'

'But Frederick said—never mind.'

She began to race back the way she'd come.

In her apartment Frederick closed the door of the cupboard he'd been exploring and said anxiously, 'I'm afraid I have found nothing.'

Daniel also closed a cupboard door. 'Nor I,' he said. 'But there hasn't been time to look everywhere. Still, I hardly expected an easy success. I doubt she's brought the letters with her; she's far too shrewd. Still, it was worth a try. Now more drastic methods will be needed.'

Frederick, a slightly puritanical young man, swallowed. 'I understand that it will be necessary for Your Majesty to make—amorous overtures to this young woman.'

An unreadable expression crossed Daniel's face, and he couldn't meet Frederick's eye. 'It would seem so,' he agreed. 'But for the sake of our country there are no lengths to which I will not go. *Ah, Miss Boothe!* How delightful to see you. But why did you hurry away so fast? Not reluctant to meet me, I hope?'

'On the contrary, I was determined to meet you,' Lizzie said, slightly breathless from running down the long corridor.

'But breakfast is for two,' Daniel said smoothly, indicating the table that had now been set up. 'Surely you realised I would be here? Frederick, you should have made the matter plain.'

Frederick murmured apologies and bowed himself out. Lizzie confronted Daniel, breathing fire.

'You actually dared to keep me prisoner!' she said. 'I don't care if you *are* a king, it was an outrageous thing to do.'

'You'll have to allow for the effects of my upbringing,' he said with a smile. 'It makes me tyrannical in small details.'

'Small—?'

'Let me pour you some orange juice. Strictly speaking, of course, you should be pouring for me, but as I don't want the jug hurled at my head I'll waive protocol this once.'

Lizzie was about to launch into her tirade again, but she found a glass pressed into her hand. She drank its contents and found them delicious.

'It was also a wasteful use of my men,' Daniel continued, seating himself and indicating for her to do the same.

'How do you mean?'

'Even without guards, you would never have left.'

'Oh, wouldn't I?'

'Of course not. Because while *you* may hold Alphonse's letters, *I* hold Liz's side of the correspondence. And you're too much of a historian to leave without trying to get a look at them.'

The truth of this struck her, making her fall briefly silent, although it was maddening to have to cede him a point.

'But I *don't* have Alphonse's letters,' she said at last. 'I told you that last night.'

'Ah, yes. A pity. We might have struck a deal.'

Lizzie's lips twitched. 'You mean, "I'll show you mine if you'll show me yours,"' she said.

'Something like that. But since you say you don't have them—'

'I don't. And the more I think of it the more I'm convinced that it can't be Auntie. She'd have told me.'

'Lizzie—'

'I think Miss Boothe is more proper, don't you?'

'Very well, Miss Boothe, the letters were written by your great-aunt. They contain details that leave no doubt.'

'But have you interpreted them correctly? If I could see what you have I might be able to point you in the right direction.'

His eyes gleamed. 'Very clever, Miss Boothe. You're a worthy opponent. Some coffee?'

'I'd rather have some letters.'

'So would I.'

'Then we seem to be at stalemate.'

'You persist in this pretence of ignorance?'

She was about to confirm this when it occurred to her that

she wasn't being very wise. If Daniel really believed she didn't have what he wanted she could be headed for a swift exit, which no longer seemed so appealing. It might be better for her to string him along. 'Always keep them wondering' had been another of Dame Elizabeth's mottoes.

After all, she argued with her conscience, she'd already told him the truth. If he chose not to believe it, was that her fault?

'What is it?' he asked, studying her face. 'Are you about to come clean after all?'

She didn't answer directly. 'Your Majesty both over- and underestimates me,' she said demurely.

'I don't—quite—understand you.'

And I'm going to keep it that way, she thought. Aloud she said, 'You credit me with more cunning than I possess, but less intelligence.'

Not a bad answer, she thought. It sounded clever, while meaning absolutely nothing. His eyes showed bafflement, as though he were seeking some deep significance in her words.

'I see,' he said at last.

You don't, she thought. *You're waving as you go down for the third time. Fine. You fooled me. Now we'll play my game.*

She spoke slowly, like someone still deciding her words, although her sharp mind was operating coolly now and her strategy was laid out.

'If you really do see,' she mused, 'then perhaps you also see that this isn't the time to talk. There are things to be considered.'

'I thought we'd already considered them. "I'll show you mine if you show me yours."'

'But yours is so much bigger than mine,' Lizzie pointed out.

'I beg your pardon!' He was startled.

'I don't just want to see letters. I wanted to browse through the archives. You have such huge archives, and I—' She shrugged self-deprecatingly.

'What you possess is valuable more for its content than its size—which, after all, isn't everything.'

'True. But don't forget I've told you that I don't have anything to trade.'

'That's true. You've *told* me.'

'But you have a good deal.'

'I am not showing you the letters.'

'I'd rather we left them for another time,' Lizzie said truthfully. 'Let's talk archives.'

'Very well,' he said, becoming businesslike. 'I'll send my archivist, Hermann Feltz, to see you. You'll find him extremely helpful. We'll talk later. Good day.'

He was gone in a moment, evidently having decided to waste no more time on her.

After that the day improved. Hermann Feltz turned out to be a charming old gentleman, eager to be helpful. He took Lizzie to the great library and placed himself at her disposal. File after file was produced at her request. The historian in Lizzie took over and she became lost in her work. They ate lunch together, talking all the time, and Hermann told her what a pleasure it was to work with someone so knowledgeable and sympathetic.

Day became evening. The old man began to yawn and Lizzie said, 'I can manage, if you'll trust me here alone.'

'The King's orders are that you're to have everything you want,' he said.

She'd guessed it, and while it pleased her it also reminded

her what a dangerous tightrope she was walking. When Daniel discovered the truth…

So what? She'd been honest from the outset. Was it her fault if he couldn't recognise the truth when he heard it?

She worked on. A meal appeared at her elbow. She thanked the footman who'd brought it and was buried in files again before he'd left the room. She spent the next hour with a morsel of food in one hand and a paper in the other, occasionally dropping the food to make a note. At last she yawned and stretched with her eyes closed. When she opened them Daniel was standing there.

'Still at work?' he asked.

'There's so much to get through, and it's all such good stuff,' she said happily. 'I can't tear myself away.'

'Don't worry, it will still be here tomorrow. It's time you stopped for the night.'

'Good heavens! After midnight. I lost track of time. It's fascinating, all those social reforms he promoted—'

'Social reforms?'

'Yes, I'm working on the fifties now. All those new laws— everyone thought the King was putting the brakes on, trying to maintain the status quo, but actually he was urging the Prime Minister on behind the scenes. He did so much good that he's never been given the credit for—'

'Or the blame if things had gone wrong,' Daniel observed. 'An appearance of political neutrality was useful to the King even then. But is that all you've been working on today? I thought you had other concerns.'

'Oh, his love life's interesting, of course,' Lizzie agreed in a faintly dismissive tone that she'd calculated to a nicety, 'but don't let's get it out of proportion. He was a fascinating man for many more reasons than that. I've been reading the cabinet papers for 1955, and guess what I found—here, look at this—'

He settled beside her and followed her pointing finger. 'That's misleading,' he said when she'd explained what had attracted her attention. 'My grandfather never meant it that way, but the Prime Minister explained it badly in cabinet, and once they'd seized the idea—'

He talked on, fetching more files for her. They argued. She talked about the lessons of history. He told her she didn't know any history worth knowing. He accused her of jumping to conclusions, she accused him of having a narrow point of view. Lizzie grew heated, hammering home her point with a fierce enthusiasm that he would have called unfeminine but for the burning, beautiful light in her eyes.

'No, listen,' she said, interrupting him with a lack of protocol that would have made his courtiers faint, 'you've got this wrong, and there's a document in the Public Records Office that proves it.'

'And what does a British office know about King Alphonse?'

'It's got all the cabinet records of that year, including his contacts with Sir Winston Churchill, and there's a memo that says—' She was away again, barely pausing for breath and not allowing him to get a word in edgeways for five minutes.

'Is it my turn now?' he asked at last.

'You're not listening to me.'

'I'm not doing anything else,' he said, exasperated to the point of raising his voice. 'Now, look, read this again—'

They were still at it, hammer and tongs when the clock struck two, amazing them both.

'Enough for tonight,' he said.

'Yes,' she agreed. She was standing, but she sat abruptly, yawning and running her hands through her hair, which had grown untidy.

Daniel regarded her, remembering the perfectly groomed woman of the ball. Now her face was bare of make-up, her eyes were drooping and she was too weary to be putting out her charms to seduce him. And that made her more mysteriously seductive than ever. As king, Daniel was used to women being consciously alluring for his benefit, their attractions all for show and not a thought in their heads but expensive gifts for themselves or advancement for their husbands. One who discarded politeness to argue with him for the sake of intellectual truth, and whose mental activity had tired her to the point of vulnerability, was new to him. She was suddenly far more intriguing than any woman in the world, and he had an urge to kiss her that was almost overwhelming.

Gently he took her hands and drew her to her feet. She opened her eyes and looked at him vaguely. 'Time to go to bed,' she sighed.

The words could have been provocative, but there was nothing teasing in the way they were said, and that provoked him more than anything. He fought his desire down. Not now, but later, when the time was right. And he would personally see to it that there *was* a right time. Whatever other disputes were between them it was growing clearer by the minute that she had to be his. He'd seen her as a woman of the world, boldly challenging him with her sexual promise. Tonight she'd been an academic, driven by an obsession with knowledge. Now the eyes that looked sleepily into his were as innocent as a child's. There had to be a way of reconciling those three aspects into the same woman.

Slipping an arm about her waist, he went to a concealed door that led into a bare wooden passage. It would take them directly to her room, and it was better that nobody saw them together like this.

At the door to her room he stopped and pushed her gently inside.

'Hey, I didn't know there was a secret passage here,' she said, waking up a little. 'Anyone could come in without my knowing.'

'Not if you slide the bolt across, like this,' he said, showing her a small gilt bolt that was almost hidden in the rest of the giltwork. 'There's another one at the bottom, and once they're shut you're completely safe from intruders.'

She didn't answer, only smiled at him in a way that threatened his good resolutions. He bid her a hurried goodnight, and quickly returned along the passage. As he went he heard the bolts slide across her door, and wondered if he'd just succumbed to a form of insanity. On the whole, he was inclined to believe that he had.

She breakfasted alone and went to the library as soon as she'd finished. Feltz wasn't there. Instead she found a boy of about twelve, who rose as soon as he saw her.

'Excuse me,' he said with a small bow. 'I was just leaving.'

He was so like Daniel that she had no trouble identifying him.

'You must be Prince Felix,' she said.

'Please, I am simply Felix,' he said, inclining his head again. He was like a little old man, she thought. It was charming, but it was also unnatural.

'I know who you are,' he went on. 'You are the lady everyone is talking about.'

'I didn't know that.'

'Only they do it very quietly. If anyone mentions you in front of my father he gets angry and tells them to be silent,' the child confided. 'But you won't tell him I said that?' he added quickly.

'Don't worry, I'll keep mum,' she promised.

He frowned. 'Mum?'

'It means keep quiet.'

He gave her a wide smile. 'Thank you. May I join you in here? I promise not to trouble you.'

'Of, course you can stay. But it's summer. Shouldn't you be outside? It's the school holiday. But I don't suppose you go to school.'

'Oh yes, I go to a school here in the city. But I have a holiday assignment to complete.'

'Don't you get any fun?'

'But of course.' He seemed mildly shocked. 'Each afternoon we go horse riding—'

'We?'

'My brother Sandor and my sister Elsa.'

'You go riding together every afternoon? Without fail?'

'Yes, and we enjoy it very much.'

'Yes, but—' To Lizzie it sounded regimented, however much they liked it, but she backed off from trying to explain to this grave child.

'Do you enjoy riding, Miss Boothe?'

'A lot.'

'I'll have the head groom find a suitable horse for you, and you can join us this afternoon. Goodbye until then.' Despite his youth the boy's manner was calmly authoritative, and she was reminded uncannily of Daniel. This child was like him in more than looks.

She worked until one o'clock, when lunch was brought to her. Afterwards a footman came to inform her that the Crown Prince was waiting for her, and led her to the stables. Felix was there, with a younger boy with a cherubic face and a girl of about ten with the beginnings of beauty. They greeted Lizzie politely, and the girl showed her some hard hats, inviting her to take her pick.

The mare they'd chosen for her was a delight, a docile creature with gentle eyes and a silken mouth. When Lizzie had spent a few moments getting introduced they were off, with a groom riding just behind.

The palace grounds were huge, with the neat gardens giving way to a park where the atmosphere was more relaxed. They gathered speed and galloped in the direction of the water. It turned out to be a lake, with a tiny pebble beach, where they dismounted to let the horses drink. The children took it in turns to ask her courteous questions, and soon Lizzie began to find their perfect behaviour slightly oppressive. To lighten the atmosphere, she said,

'I knew a lake like this when I was a child. It was in the local park and I used to compete with the boys in stone throwing. I could beat them too.'

'Stone throwing?' Felix echoed with a little frown.

'Like this.' She picked up a pebble, checked to see that there was no passing wildlife to be endangered, took careful aim, and sent the stone skimming across the surface of the water until it reached the other side.

'Try it,' she suggested.

Felix did so, but he couldn't manage the flick of the wrist

that causing the skimming action. He threw 'straight' and the
stone dropped into the water with a miserable 'plop'. Sandor
had no better luck.

'Now you,' Lizzie said to Elsa.

'Me?'

'What they can do, you can do. And, if you're like me, you
can probably do it better.'

And she did. With sharper eyes than her brothers Elsa had
noticed the crucial wrist movement, and with her first throw
she made the stone bounce along the surface of the water. Not
far, but enough to goad her brothers out of their perfect behaviour, Lizzie was glad to notice.

Sandor was the next to get the idea. Of the three he seemed
the most naturally aggressive. He threw and threw, his face
creased into a scowl that threatened a temper if he wasn't ac-
knowledged the winner. The gentle Felix did his best, but he
was the first to stop when a duck suddenly appeared, followed
by frantically paddling ducklings.

'Wait,' Lizzie said urgently. 'You might hurt one of them.'

'Let them get out of the way,' Sandor blustered.

'I said *wait*,' Lizzie insisted, taking firm hold of the hand
he was raising.

Sandor threw her a black look but, reading the determina-
tion in her eyes, backed down. The other two children ex-
changed glances.

Lizzie had feared a tantrum from a child who was clearly
used to getting his own way. But the next moment Sandor had
shrugged the matter aside and was all smiles. He even began
to clown, calling to the duck across the water,

'Excuse me, dear madam, would you mind hurrying,
please?'

The mother duck cast him a startled look and began paddling faster, which made them all burst out laughing, Sandor loudest of all.

'Good afternoon.'

Nobody had known that Daniel was there, and at the sound of his voice they all swung around, their laughter fading to silence. Lizzie knew a stab of pity for him. It must be terrible for any man to know that his presence was a blight on his children.

And he did know. She could see it in his eyes, although his pleasant smile never wavered as they greeted him. He was their father, but first of all he was their king, and he was no more skilled than they at finding a way around that.

He asked about their ride and they responded with appropriate words. Lizzie did her best to help, praising the children as good hosts, he congratulated them, and they were all relieved when it was over.

The children continued their ride with the groom. Daniel looked at her, frowning.

'How did you contrive to meet my children?' he asked curtly. 'They can't tell you anything.'

Lizzie's eyes flashed. 'You've got a nerve, suggesting I wormed my way in. I didn't "contrive" anything. I don't stoop to those methods.'

'Then how did you meet them?'

'Felix was ahead of me in the library this morning. We introduced ourselves and he invited me to ride with them.'

He closed his eyes tiredly. 'Forgive me. I didn't mean to be rude. I'm afraid I grow suspicious of everything. Ride with me.'

She mounted the mare and the two horses began to walk side by side.

'Your children are charming,' she ventured.

'They are also afraid of me,' he said in a brooding voice.

'A little in awe, perhaps, but not afraid.'

'I haven't known what to say to them since their mother died.'

Lizzie could believe it all too easily. 'What was she like?' she asked gently.

'She was a wonderful mother,' Daniel said at once. 'She insisted on taking charge of the nursery herself. She left the nannies very little to do. She said that nobody must come between her and her children.'

Lizzie wondered if he knew what he was revealing. Daniel had nothing but good to say of his late wife, but through the words there appeared a picture of a woman who had not loved her husband and had consoled herself with her children. He gave no hint as to whether he had loved Serena, but it was clear that her remoteness had left him lonelier. The right woman could have drawn him out, she thought, encouraged the warmth that she was sure was there in him. If she'd loved him…

Lizzie pulled herself together, wondering where her wits were wandering. It was Daniel's fault for looking so handsome as they drifted beneath the trees, moving in and out of the sunlight. He wore no jacket and his sleeves were short, leaving no doubt of the spare, hard lines of his body, the broad chest and narrow hips. He controlled his horse easily, with slight movements of his muscular thighs that held her attention even while she knew that a wise woman would blank him out, for her own sake.

It was a shame, she thought. So much masculine power and beauty was destined for an athlete, a dancer, or a trapeze artist. One thing was for sure. It was wasted on a king.

CHAPTER FOUR

THAT night Lizzie was about to go to bed when there was a knock on the door to the secret passage.

'It's Daniel,' came a quiet voice from behind.

She slid back the bolts and he stepped into the room, still in white tie and tails from a reception at a foreign embassy. He looked pale and drawn, as though his mind was troubled.

'I've brought you something,' he said, giving her a large brown envelope.

'The letters,' she breathed, exploring.

'Four of them, to start with. You might tell me if you recognise Dame Elizabeth's writing.'

She settled down on the sofa and began to go through them like a treasure hunter who'd just struck gold.

'I don't really know her writing,' she said regretfully. 'In her last years she had arthritis in her hands and never wrote anything down if she could help it. This could be hers. I'm not sure.'

The letters were touching. A gentle, eager soul breathed through the words. This was a woman with a great, tender heart, full of love for one man.

'My goodness,' she breathed. 'I'd really love to—' She

checked herself on the verge of saying she'd love to see the other side of the correspondence. It would be silly to throw away her ace while she was winning.

'Love to—?' Daniel asked.

'Love to see the rest of the letters.'

'This is all you get for the moment.'

She began to read the four letters slowly. They were not only loving but also frankly sensual in a way that made her revise her opinion of Alphonse.

'I wish I'd known your grandfather,' she murmured. 'He can't have been the stick-in-the-mud everyone thought, or no woman would have written to him like this.'

'I beg your pardon!' Daniel said frostily. 'I resent the term "stick-in-the-mud".'

'Sorry,' Lizzie said quickly. 'But you know what I mean.'

'I don't think I do. He was a man I greatly admired—'

'But don't you realise that now you've got another reason to admire him? If he could inspire this kind of love he must have been quite a man. Listen…'

'"*You have given me a reason to live. We are so far apart and see each other so little, and yet you are with me every moment because you're never absent from my heart.*"'

From another letter Lizzie read, '"*I can feel you with me now, your body against mine, your loving still part of me, and I wonder how I lived before we met. To me the world is a beautiful place because you are in it. Whatever happens from now on, I shall say my life was worthwhile, because I was loved by you.*"'

She stopped. After a moment some quality in the silence made her look up to find him staring into space. He looked stunned.

'Daniel,' she said, laying her hand over his.

He didn't look at her. His eyes were fixed on something she couldn't see. Perhaps his grandfather. Perhaps himself.

'I read that letter earlier,' he murmured. 'But I barely noticed those words. When you read them—it's different—I hear them for the first time—almost as though you—'

He stopped, suddenly self-conscious.

'You're right,' he went on after a moment. 'How little I really knew him! I admired him, but I was in awe of him, just as my own children are of me. He seemed so stiff and remote. But he couldn't have been if a woman could write such words to him.'

He gave a wry laugh. 'What do we ever know of another person? I wanted to be like him, and now I discover that I never can be. He was a man who could inspire a woman to say that the world was beautiful because of him. And I know, if I'm honest, that no woman has ever said or even thought that about me.'

'What about your wife?' Lizzie asked.

'I married when I was nineteen. She was twenty-four. We weren't in love. It was a state marriage, and we were raised to the idea of duty.'

'But didn't you ever fall in love?'

'She was in love with someone else. We didn't talk about it. Now I look back, we didn't talk about anything, which may be why we managed to remain on cordial terms until she died. If people don't talk to each other, there's nothing to quarrel about.'

'You poor soul,' Lizzie said, meaning it.

'She's the one you should feel sorry for. She was forced to separate from the man she loved and marry a silly boy. She suffered an arid marriage with only her children to console her, and died before her life could get any better.'

'How did she die?'

'A fall from her horse. She was a reckless rider. Maybe she was trying to ease the frustrations of her life.' He gave a bitter laugh, directed at himself. 'You should have heard my romantic notions as a bridegroom. Despite the odds, I'd convinced myself that we might fall in love. I'd have gladly loved her. She was beautiful. But the other man was always there in her heart, and I never had a chance.'

'Did you know who he was?'

'Oh, yes, he was a splendid fellow, just right for her. A nervous teenager had no chance of winning her heart. I honour her for her fidelity to me. I know she never wavered. But, poor woman, it was a bleak business for her!'

'And for you,' Lizzie said sympathetically.

The picture he'd painted for her was vivid: the lonely boy, longing for some love in a world that had given him none and finding only a wife as deprived as himself. The handsome, apparently confident man before her was a shell. Inside him the 'nervous teenager' still lived, and probably always would, unless another woman's touch could heal his wounds.

Thinking of nothing but to comfort him, she laid her hand on his cheek, searching his face. He raised his eyes to hers and she was shocked at their defencelessness. They were on his ground. By all the rules he should be in control. But something in that letter had broken his control by revealing his own loneliness to him in cruel colours. No woman found the world beautiful because he was in it, and the knowledge broke his heart. Now he was reaching out blindly to her in his need, and she responded with her own need.

For she was as vulnerable as he. Bess had said she was too armoured, implying that if she didn't soon give a man her heart—all of it, with nothing held back—Lizzie was in danger of becoming hard. Her head told her that Daniel could never be the right man. She'd meant only to entice him into letting her win their duel of wits, but suddenly everything was different. She ached for him. She longed to ease his sadness, and everything went down before that. All self forgotten, caring only for him, she put her arms about him.

His own arms went about her at once, and they stood together in a long, close embrace. At first he didn't try to kiss her, but buried his face against her as though finding there some long sought refuge.

'Lizzie,' he whispered, then again, 'Lizzie, Lizzie…' Just her name repeated over and over, as though the very sound was a spell to ward off evil.

It was sweet to hold him, feeling the warmth of his body mingle with her own, and for the moment that was all she asked. Then she felt the change that came over him as his lips found her neck and began to bestow soft kisses. She sighed with pleasure and began to wreathe her fingers in his hair, turning her neck this way and that to tempt his mouth.

Lower the trail went, down her neck to her almost exposed breasts in the low-cut nightdress, lower still, lower, and every fibre of her being was crying *yes*. She would be cautious another time. This was the man she wanted.

He raised his head. She could feel him trembling. 'You make it very hard to remember that I'm a man of honour,' he growled.

'Perhaps you remember that too often. Is being a man of honour so important?'

'It has to be—it must be—' he said, as if trying to convince himself. He took her face between his hands, speaking softly and with sincerity. 'Lizzie, will you believe me? I didn't come here tonight meaning this to happen.'

'Yes, I believe you.' It was true. Beneath the regimented exterior was a man who could be impulsive. 'It doesn't matter. Don't plan everything. Let things happen to you. It'll be all right. Trust me—trust me—'

And then she felt him freeze suddenly.

'What did you say?' he asked in a strange voice.

'Trust me.' She kissed him playfully. 'Don't you think you could trust me now?'

Bewildered, she knew that a change had come over him. He almost snatched his hand out of hers.

'It isn't that,' he said, sounding as though he spoke with difficulty. 'But I—I really shouldn't be here. This isn't right.'

'I see.' Her eyes flashed. 'Then you don't trust me. How stupid of me to forget.'

'Lizzie, please, it isn't that. It's just that I—I can't explain.'

'Or you don't need to. You lured me here as an enemy, and I'm still an enemy, aren't I? What a pity you confided so much to me tonight. And me a historian! Who knows who I'll tell? Or what indiscreet notes I might make.'

He was pale. 'Will you?'

'Of course not. *You shouldn't have asked me that!*'

'I didn't mean to. I don't know what came over me—at least, I can't explain—'

'I think you already have.'

His tone became more distant. 'There's still a lot we don't know about each other, and perhaps we should both be careful.'

She matched his distant tone with one of her own. 'I think Your Majesty had better leave.'

'Yes, perhaps I should.'

He gave her a small, correct little bow, and went out through the secret door.

She hurried after him and slammed the bolts shut. Then she leaned against the door, resisting the impulse to call him back.

The next morning Frederick brought her a large bag containing the rest of Liz's letters, explaining that he was acting on the King's instructions. His Majesty had left the palace unexpectedly to visit Helmand, his private estate a hundred miles away, and would be gone for some time.

After that she lived in limbo. She didn't know how long Daniel would be away, or whether he meant her to leave before he returned. She only knew that she was furious with him, insulted by him, and yearned for him.

The letters were a goldmine, but a frustrating one. Liz must surely be Dame Elizabeth, since the pattern of her life seemed to follow the Dame's so exactly. But although there were a thousand hints, there was still no certainty.

The more she read the more she longed for Daniel to be there. There was such love in these pages, and with every passing day she felt an affinity with the writer. 'Liz' had seen an aching need beneath Alphonse's forbidding exterior that had called forth her love and protectiveness. That was their secret. In the world's eyes he was a man of power, but it was she who had protected him.

Daniel was Daniel and not Alphonse, and history never actually repeated itself. But he'd been moulded by the same conditions as his grandfather and left emotionally adrift in the

same way. And she knew now that something in him had
called to her from the first moment.

Several times she rode with the children. They seemed to
like her, and she found them increasingly easy to talk to.
Even Sandor's quicksilver temper was controlled in her
presence, Elsa was showing signs of a pretty wit, and Felix
was beginning to come out of his shell.

They were walking through the woods one afternoon, with
Sandor telling them all a funny story, when a sound made
them all look up. Daniel was walking through the trees. He
wore an informal opennecked shirt, and had something in his
arms that squealed and squirmed. Closer inspection revealed
it to be three puppies, each about eight weeks.

'A bitch whelped in the Helmand stables a while back,' he
said. 'Here you are. One each. Now, be off with you.'

Shouting joyfully, the children took charge of the wrig-
gling bundles, and scampered away.

Daniel stood looking at Lizzie. She hadn't taken her eyes
from him since the first moment. Nor had she been able to
move. But suddenly movement returned to her. He opened
his arms and she threw herself into them.

'I've missed you,' he said between kisses. 'I went away
from you, but it did no good. You came with me. You've been
with me all the while. You won't go away.'

It was the same with her, and she knew he understood her
without words.

'You're in my heart for always,' he said. 'At first I thought
you might leave while I was gone, and it would be better for
both of us if you did. But this morning I awoke in the early
hours and I was so afraid in case you'd left that I had to come
home. Kiss me, *kiss me*.'

She responded wholeheartedly, throwing her arms about his neck and giving herself up to the sensation of loving and being loved.

'I've so much to say to you, Lizzie, and you—have you nothing to say to me?'

'Oh, yes, so much.' She took his hand and began to draw him deeper into the wood.

But when he took her in his arms again she discovered that there was nothing to say, or at least nothing that couldn't wait. They clung together like people who'd narrowly avoided falling into an abyss.

A giggle from nearby made them both swing around quickly.

'What are you three—?' Daniel began to yell. Then the urgent pressure of Lizzie's hands checked him. 'I thought you'd gone,' he said, sounding resigned.

'We're sorry, sir,' Felix said quickly. His laugh had faded and he looked anxious.

'You're not annoyed, are you?' Lizzie muttered, so softly that only he could hear.

'No, I'm not annoyed.' Something about their tense faces seemed to get through to him because he added quickly, 'I'm not angry. Really.'

They visibly relaxed and the smiles began to creep back to their faces, but cautiously, as though ready to vanish again in an instant.

'We came back to say thank you for the puppies,' Sandor said.

'Have fun with them. But you look after them yourselves. You feed them, clean up after them.'

Sandor frowned. 'But there are servants—'

'No servants, *you* do it.' Then Daniel grew still and raised his head, as though listening for silent music in the air. Lizzie held her breath, sure that she knew the thought that had come to him. She was certain of it when he added, 'If you don't feed those dogs, nobody does. So their lives are in your hands.'

The children nodded eagerly and raced off. But when they'd gone Daniel frowned, saying, 'Why did I say that? Of course they haven't got time to—'

'Yes, they have,' Lizzie said, clasping his hand. 'You did the right thing. Perhaps we'd better get back.'

'Yes, we don't want any more little spies,' he said, moving off, still with her hand in his.

That evening she dined with Daniel and the children. It was a happy party, with everyone more relaxed than Lizzie had ever seen them. They kept to safe topics, like dog care, and to Lizzie's surprise Daniel proved an expert.

'I had to care for my own dog when I was a child,' he explained.

'But suppose you had to be away, sir?' Felix asked, frowning.

Daniel winced. 'I'd rather you didn't call me sir.'

'But you've never said anything before,' Sandor pointed out. He looked surprised. 'I've never noticed before.'

'But what shall we say instead?' Elsa wanted to know.

That confused them, making Lizzie realise that the next step was still a big one.

'Let's sort it out later,' she said quickly. 'Felix wants to know what you did about the puppy when you were away.'

'Then I could delegate someone to do it for me, but it was my job to pick them and explain everything.'

'Father!' Sandor said suddenly. 'Or Poppa. Or Papa.'

'Dad? Daddy?' Lizzie said, then cunningly corrected herself, 'No, I shouldn't have said that. They're *much* too informal. Quite improper.'

'Not at all,' Daniel said at once.

They finally settled on Dad for the boys and Daddy for Elsa. Daniel's eyes met Lizzie's across the table, silently smiling, telling her he understood her little trick.

When the youngsters had gone to bed Daniel said, 'Did you get what I left you?'

'The rest of the letters? Yes, thank you. It was wonderful of you.'

'Did you make anything of them?'

'A good deal, and I think you did too.'

He shrugged. 'I must confess I haven't read them all in detail, just well enough for a general idea of what they were.'

'I think you noticed more than you realise.'

'What do you mean?'

'Come with me and I'll show you.'

In her room she unlocked the drawer where she kept all the letters, and took out one of the first. 'Tell me about the dog you looked after,' she said.

'He was called Tiger. A stupid name because he was just a scruffy mongrel who wandered in one day and attached himself to me. You should have heard the commotion. Only a pedigree animal was suitable for the Crown Prince. But my grandfather let me keep him. He said—'

'Yes?' Lizzie asked.

Speaking as in a dream, Daniel replied, 'He said, "He's your responsibility. If you don't feed him, nobody else will. His life is in your hands." So that's why—today, when I said those words—'

'You were remembering when you last heard them.'

'Yes, I see that, but what does this have to do with a letter?'

'Look at that,' she said, holding one out to him. 'Halfway down the page.'

And there it was, in Liz's words.

> *You talk about teaching Daniel responsibility, but you mean lectures and theory. Give the poor child a dog and let him choose it for himself. He will learn more about responsibility from a creature he loves, and who depends on him entirely, than from all the lessons in books.*

'So that was why he did it,' Daniel said, sitting slowly on the bed, his attention riveted on the paper in his hand. 'It came from her. Then I'm in her debt for years of happiness. And she was right, of course. It was all here, but when I first glanced over this letter I missed it.'

'You weren't ready. Not like now.'

'I really hope Liz is your great-aunt. Not that there's any real doubt of it, but I'm beginning to understand so much—how he depended on her. She must have been the most important person in his life, just as you—' He stopped and looked at her. 'Lizzie, darling, I'm not imagining this, am I?'

'Imagination?' she teased. 'You?'

'No, I haven't much. So I couldn't have imagined that you feel for me as I feel for you. Could I?' He was pleading.

'No,' she said seriously, 'you didn't imagine that.'

He dropped the letter so that it fell, unheeded, to the floor. He seized her against him like a man just released from prison. His kisses too had the desperation of sudden freedom, shot through with dread lest the precious gift be snatched away. And behind that lay the eagerness of a boy exploring love, almost as a new adventure. She kissed him back in reassurance, but gradually that gave way to the thrills that were coursing through her. He was the man she loved, but he was also the most sexually attractive male animal that it had ever been her privilege to encounter. She'd sensed that at the ball, when she'd first felt his arms about her, and everything since then had been a matter of waiting to tie up the loose ends.

Suddenly he stopped, holding her face between his two hands, whispering, 'Are you sure? Are you quite sure, Lizzie? Don't feel you have to just because I—because of this place and all the trappings.'

She loved him for his doubts. In the past he'd shown her the arrogance of power. Now he trusted her with the humility deep inside him.

'Are you sure?' he repeated again. 'It has to be *me*, for myself alone. I don't want it any other way.'

'Just you,' she promised. 'There's nobody else in my heart, and there never will be again.'

She slipped out of her robe and nightdress so that he could see all the beauty she brought him. She knew her nakedness was magnificent, but at this moment she only cared for it as a gift for the lonely, doubt-ridden man who'd taken refuge in her heart.

And it would be a true refuge for him, she vowed as he lay down beside her on the bed. Whatever the future held, whatever price she had to pay for loving him—and it might be a great one—she would say it was all worth it if she could give him any happiness.

From the way he made love she could tell that the last of

his doubts still lingered. There was about him a serious in-
tentness that was beautiful here and now. But far back in her
mind she made a note that in future she must teach him how
to be a little light-hearted.

No woman could have asked for a more tender or consid-
erate loving, but beneath it she could sense the vigour, sternly
leashed back for her sake. The knowledge was a new excitement, a promise for the future. Next time they made love he
wouldn't hold it back; she would see to that. But for now they
were getting introduced, delighting in what they found, joyful
in each other. Only at the last moment did his passion slip
beyond his control, and he claimed her with a fierceness that
she willingly matched.

There was a long silence then, broken only by breathing
and the soft sound of their heartbeats fading. Daniel kissed
her and drew her close.

'Thank you,' he murmured.

She gave a chuckle, full of pleasure and satisfaction. 'I
think I should be thanking you. That was the nicest thing
that's ever happened to me.'

'I want to toast you in champagne.'

'So let's send for some.'

'You mean I should make the call from your room? That
would really give them something to talk about.'

'No, I will.' She lifted the house phone and made the order.
'You stay here while I wait for it in the sitting room.'

The champagne arrived five minutes later. Lizzie dressed
soberly and closed the door into her bedroom.

'There's only one glass,' she said, bringing everything in
a moment later. 'I could hardly ask for two, but I think there
are some in that cupboard.' She eyed him, lying naked on

the tumbled bed. 'If you lie like that I shall forget all about champagne.'

'Good,' he said, grinning. 'Why are you wearing so much?'

She laughed and tossed her clothes aside while he poured two glasses.

They toasted each other, then Daniel said, 'There must be something else. Let's drink to a bargain well sealed. Except that you haven't kept your side yet.'

'How do you mean?' she asked, trying to sound casual, although she sensed doom creeping up on her. However she'd pictured the moment of truth, it hadn't been like this.

'"I'll show you mine if you'll show me yours,"' he quoted. 'That was the deal. What have you done with Alphonse's letters? Oh, never mind; I'm feeling too happy to worry about that. I just want to think about you. Tomorrow will do for the letters.'

'Yes,' she said, relieved. 'Tomorrow.'

But something in her voice struck his ears strangely. He frowned and looked curiously at her face.

'You have got them safe, haven't you, darling?'

Oh, heck! she thought. Why now?

'You have, haven't you, Lizzie?'

'I thought you said you didn't want to talk about this now?'

'Yes, but you've got me worried. *Lizzie*—'

'Daniel, I told you right from the start that I don't have those letters.'

He looked at her quizzically. 'But of course you have them. You as good as told me—' He caught her eye and said slowly, 'What have we been talking about all this time?'

She took the precaution of rising and moving away, unaware that her shape was distracting Daniel from what he was pursuing. Almost, but not quite.

'Evidently we haven't been talking about the same thing,' she observed.

'You knew I was offering a bargain.'

'And you knew I didn't have them. I told you that in this very room.'

'Yes, but then you—' He rose from the bed and began to follow her. 'Then you—'

'Eased up on the denials a little,' she told him, bland-faced.

He advanced purposefully on her. 'You scheming, two-faced little—'

She backed away. 'Now Daniel—'

'*Your Majesty!*'

'Rats! If you want to be called Your Majesty, put something on first.'

'Don't change the subject.'

She chuckled. 'There's only one subject that interests me at the moment. You too, from the look of it.'

One glance down at himself was enough to make him accept the inevitable.

'We'll talk later,' he muttered, lifting her right off her feet and tossing her so that she landed sprawling on the bed.

'All right, my love,' she gasped as he dived and landed on top of her. 'Anything that you—mmm!'

CHAPTER FIVE

SHE began a double life. By day she was the historian working seriously on the Voltavian archives. If she met Daniel in the presence of anyone else she would address him as 'Your Majesty' the first time, and 'sir' after that, as did his courtiers.

But at night she called him Daniel, and laughed as she melted in his arms. Their loving was passionate, and full of joy, and afterwards, as he lay sleeping in her arms—for he always slept first—she would hold him protectively and wonder if this was how Liz had felt with Alphonse. And then she knew that was impossible, because no woman in the world had felt the special joy that was hers.

After the first explosion he'd accepted the fact that she couldn't produce Alphonse's letters with wry humour. It delighted her that he had managed to laugh about it.

'You got the better of me,' he said without rancour. 'But you wait and see. I'll get even.'

'I'm looking forward to it,' she teased.

When she was there he could enjoy a family evening, and even displayed a talent for playing the piano that none of his children had known about before.

They confided this to her when Daniel was out of earshot. They revealed also, without exactly knowing they were doing so, that their mother had drummed into their head that he was their king first and their father second. With herself, she had stressed, it was the other way around.

Daniel might regard his late wife generously but Lizzie's thoughts were less charitable. Serena had been so possessive about her children that she'd bolstered her own position at her husband's expense, and everyone was suffering for it now.

Once, when the palace was quiet, he showed her where he lived, and she was struck by the contrast between the magnificent bedroom where the king officially slept and the little monastic cell where he actually passed his nights—those that he didn't spend with her.

'Who's this?' she asked, looking at a small painting on the wall. It showed a man in Voltavian military uniform, but with a gentle, unmilitary face, on the verge of a smile.

'That's my great-uncle, Carl. Alphonse's younger brother. He was a dear fellow, everybody loved him. There's a story that the only reason Alphonse married Princess Irma was to clear the way for Carl to marry the woman he loved. She was the daughter of a lawyer, respectable and a lady, but this was seventy years ago, when it was unthinkable for a prince to make such a marriage. And Carl was next in line to the throne, after Alphonse.

'So Alphonse married and had a son, and then the way was clear for Carl. He renounced his rights of succession, married his lady, and they lived very happily for fifty years.'

'What a charming story. And Alphonse really made a dutiful marriage just to help Carl?'

'So they say. My grandfather would never confirm or deny

it. But Carl was very dear to him, and his happiest times were spent visiting the family. Mine too. They always seemed so happy. Carl was a wise man to marry where his heart led him.'

'But he did it at someone else's expense,' Lizzie pointed out. 'Your grandfather couldn't have done the same. Nor could you.'

Daniel was studying the picture. 'I think I could—now,' he said. 'I've made one state marriage, given my country three children. Next time I shall please myself.'

He wasn't looking at her as he spoke—almost deliberately, it seemed to her. She drew a sharp breath at what he might be implying, but before she could reply a buzzer went to summon him to deal with an unexpected crisis. Lizzie had to leave and it was the following evening before she saw him.

He didn't raise the matter again, and she wondered if she'd misunderstood him. Or perhaps he really had meant what she hoped, and then caution had checked him. The thought that they might actually be able to marry was too wonderful to be believed. She wouldn't let herself dwell on it.

Their secret life was charmingly domestic, although Daniel observed that it sometimes made him feel like a character in a French farce. In the morning she was always the first up, slipping out to the sitting room where the newspapers had been quietly laid out by Frederick. Breakfast of rolls and orange juice was served in the same fashion, with Daniel discreetly out of sight behind the bedroom door. And if anyone noticed that Lizzie's food consumption had recently doubled, nobody mentioned it.

They would enjoy breakfast together, lingering until the last moment, until he had to present himself to his court and she must go to the library, and they would look forward to their meeting in the afternoon when they rode with his children.

The morning papers came in three languages, and while with Lizzie Daniel would particularly enjoy reading the English ones, giving some trenchant opinions on what he read there.

'You should see what they say here,' he said one morning. 'I know there isn't a word of truth in it, but what can I—? Lizzie? My darling? What is it?'

She forced herself out of a sad dream and gave him a forced smile. 'Nothing,' she said.

'Don't say "nothing" when it makes you look like that.'

'All right.' She showed him what she'd been reading. The picture of a handsome young man, with a daredevil face, stared out from the paper. The caption read, *Toby Wrenworth killed in motorcycle race.*

Daniel felt as though something had struck him in the chest. He could barely force himself to ask, 'He means something to you, this man?'

'He did once. We were married for a couple of years.'

'Married?'

'I was eighteen and he was handsome and dashing. Auntie warned me against it, but I wouldn't listen. I was so sure I could make him settle down. Of course he didn't. He got bored and took off, and we were divorced. He was only happy taking insane risks. It was only a matter of time before this happened.'

'Did you stay in touch?'

'No. I haven't spoken to him for years. It was all over long ago.'

'But he's remained in your heart?' He was watching her face intently.

'Not him so much as the memories of the happiness we shared. But it was a very short happiness. I was a stupid, ignorant girl or I'd have known I couldn't change him.'

He wished he'd known that stupid, ignorant girl who'd given her whole heart to a man who hadn't valued it. What had she been like in the flush of her first love? His longing to know that, to have been the man who inspired her first young passion, was so intense that for a moment he couldn't speak.

'Don't,' he said, tossing the paper aside and taking her face between his hands. 'Forget him. Look at me.'

She did so, and tried to smile. But it was an unconvincing smile and she saw the shadow of fear cross his face.

'It's all right,' she tried to reassure him. 'I just need to be alone for a while.'

'I have to go, but I'll see you this afternoon—hell, no, I've got meetings all day, and tonight I have to attend the opera.'

'Late tonight, then,' she said.

She spent the day wandering alone in the woods, thinking about Toby. The boy she'd known had been gone even before his death; she could see that from the face in the paper. It was a hard-bitten man who looked out from the front page, and the text made it clear that he'd cared for nothing and nobody except riding his powerful machine in races. Somewhere in the background was a discarded girlfriend and two illegitimate children. The Dame had been right all along. All teeth and trousers. And selfish with it.

Toby had changed her, teaching her the value of keeping her heart to herself, and so, in his way, he'd helped to bring her to this point. She had a heart to give to the one man who mattered, because after that first fling she'd never wasted it again. Her sadness was all for Toby, who'd loved life and lost it while she was preparing to move on to a new life.

It was nearly two in the morning before Daniel came to her, and she could see in his face that his day had been wretched. Years had left him skilled in concealing his feelings, but now they burst out in the first moment.

'Tell me the worst,' he said harshly. 'You still love him, don't you? You've been trying to put him behind you, but you can't.'

'Darling, that's not true.'

'I think it is. That's why you play with men so easily—because you couldn't have the one who mattered. But who do you make love with? When you lie in my arms whose face do you see?'

Suddenly she understood. 'No, you've got it all wrong,' she said, giving him a little shake. 'It isn't happening again, I promise. I'm not Serena, pining for another man.'

He gave a shaky laugh. 'Am I that transparent?'

'Just a little.'

'I thought you were all mine. If I discovered that you weren't, my life would be dark again. And that would be hard to bear when you've shown me the light.'

'I *am* all yours,' she promised. 'I've been over Toby for years. It was just a shock to read about his death like that. I don't dream of him. I dream of you.'

He relaxed in her arms and allowed himself to be reassured. Instead of taking him straight to bed Lizzie ordered a light meal and they sat and talked about nothing very much. It was being together that mattered, and when she could feel that he was calmer and happier, then she took him to bed and loved him tenderly.

As they lay together afterwards he said, 'If I'd known I was going to fall in love with you, I'd have run for my life.'

'Love?' she asked in a soft murmur. 'Is this love?'

'Don't you feel that it is?'

'Yes, I do.' She buried her face against him, whispering, 'And I'm so happy now.'

Next morning he had to leave her earlier than usual for a meeting with his Prime Minister. Before going he said, 'Tonight will be special. I have a surprise for you.'

'A surprise? Oh, tell me now,' she begged eagerly.

'Then it wouldn't be a surprise. I don't want to spoil it, but it's something that will mean a lot to you.' He sighed, kissed her tenderly, and then again. 'If I don't leave you now I won't be able to. Goodbye, my darling, until tonight.'

When he'd gone she had a bracing shower. As she was drying herself her phone rang. She answered eagerly, expecting to hear Daniel's voice. But it was a stranger, and as she listened her smile faded.

She dressed quickly and called Daniel. 'I have to leave, right now,' she said.

'You can't leave me,' he said, becoming imperious in a moment. 'I won't let you go, ever. Wait there.' He hung up before she could reply.

He was with her in a moment. 'What is this nonsense about leaving?'

'I'll come back when I can, but I have a sick friend who needs me. It's Bess. I told you about her. She's had a heart attack and the hospital sent for me. I'm all she has.'

'Forgive me,' he said at once. 'I was being selfish. It's so hard to part with you when I've only just discovered you. But you must go at once. My own plane will take you—'

'No need, darling. There's a flight in an hour, and if I go now I might just catch it.'

'Don't worry. I'll call the airport. It won't leave without you.'

She gave a shaky smile. 'What it is to be a king.'

'It's only valuable to me if I can use it to make your life a little easier. But before you go there's something I want to say—you must understand—'

She waited, but after hesitating for a long moment he sighed and said, 'Never mind. This isn't the moment. But remember that I love you whatever—whatever happens.'

'Darling, whatever's the matter?'

He put his arms about her. 'Promise me that you'll return. You won't just abandon me.'

'How could I do that when I love you so much? I'll be thinking about you.'

'And I,' he said, 'will start to think about you the moment we say goodbye. Wherever you are, whatever you do, my thoughts will be with you every moment until you return.'

Felix, Sandor and Elsa came down with her to the palace car that Daniel had commanded to take her to the airport. As it drove away she looked back to see them waving, their faces anxious. Raising her eyes a little, she could see Daniel motionless at an upstairs window.

Lizzie's return to Voltavia was in stark contrast to her departure. Three days later she arrived without warning, stormed into her apartment and snatched up the telephone to call Daniel. The phone was answered by Frederick.

'Kindly tell His Majesty that I want to see him.'

Frederick's gasp was audible down the line. He knew, as everyone did, that Lizzie was privileged, but even she couldn't command the King with the snap of her fingers. He tried to explain this diplomatically, but she steamrollered over him.

'Tell him I've got what he wants,' she said sulphurously. 'That'll bring him.'

She hung up. At the other end of the line Frederick mopped his brow.

For the next few minutes Lizzie prowled her apartment like an angry lioness, wondering how her happiness could have turned to dust so quickly. Her visit to England had been marked by two discoveries, one of which had filled her with joy and wonder. The other had filled her with such profound bitterness that she wondered how she could bear to see Daniel again, ever.

But she would see him, one last time. She would give him the thing for which he had schemed and betrayed. Perhaps she would even manage to tell him what she thought of him, although it would be hard to put the depth of her misery into words. Then she would leave Voltavia and try to forget that Daniel existed.

She looked up sharply as the door opened. There he was, smiling as though nothing pleased him so much as the sight of her, although she had rudely summoned him in a way that would once have earned his displeasure. He came towards her, hands outstretched, eyes warm. Lizzie clenched her own hands, forcing herself to remember that this man had deceived her cruelly. Otherwise she might have thought he was regarding her with love.

'You came back quickly,' he said, 'just as you promised. But whatever did you say to poor Frederick to put him in such a fret?' She stared at him, bleak-eyed, and his smile died. 'What is it, my darling?'

'Don't call me that,' she said harshly. 'You can stop the pretence. I know the truth now.'

'Whatever do you mean?'

'Did you think I wouldn't find out that you had my house burgled?'

If she'd had any doubts his sharp intake of breath dispelled them. He was pale and startled, but he knew what she was taking about.

'It's true, then,' she said bitterly. 'You did it. You ordered it. And all the time you— Dear God!' The last words were a cry of anguish.

'Lizzie, please listen to me. It's not as you think.'

She rounded on him. 'Of course it is. It's exactly as I think. I was a fool, but I'm not a fool any more, so don't insult my intelligence.'

The sudden silence was harsh and ugly, unlike the sweet, companionable silences that had fallen between them so often.

'How did you know?' he asked at last, in a voice that seemed to come from a great distance.

'Your operatives were very good, but not quite good enough. A few things were out of place. I noticed because I tend to keep things as my great-aunt left them. I didn't believe it at first, but when I questioned my neighbours I learned a lot. Like that they entered by the front door. That's why nobody was alarmed. They looked so respectable.'

Her eyes were very cold as she said, 'I wondered how they got a key to my house. And then I remembered the ball, and how you danced me along the terrace, taking both my hands so that I had to leave my purse behind. You did the "heady passion" bit very well, I'll give you that. And you judged the time so well. Just long enough for someone to open my purse and take a wax impression of the key.'

She waited to see if he would answer, but he stood silent, looking at her with eyes full of pain.

'But why?' she said at last. 'You could have asked me for those letters when we first met in London. You thought I was negotiating. So why not come right out with it there and then? Why invite me here at all?

'That was the question I should have asked myself a long time ago, but I wasn't thinking straight. And why? Because of all that romantic claptrap you showered on me. There wasn't a word of truth in it. You just wanted me in a daze so that I didn't know whether I was coming or going, because that way you could keep me here as long as it suited you. And I fell for it. Me, who prides herself on her cool, logical mind. I could laugh when I remember how I actually lectured you about the lessons of history, but I forgot the most important one, didn't I? *Put not your trust in princes!*

'And all the time I was here your people were going through my house. You didn't want to buy, you wanted to steal.'

'That's not true,' he said harshly. 'I always meant to pay you for those letters, but I was afraid you might have copies, or keep some back.'

'Oh, boy, you were really thorough, weren't you? You even tried my bank. But I don't have a safety deposit box, as I gather the manager told you. Of course, there are a lot more banks to try. Who knows what I might be hiding in some little out-of-the-way branch—?'

'Stop!' he said harshly. 'I deserve all you say of me, but let me tell you the truth—'

'You don't deal in truth. You're a king; you have other priorities. You as good as warned me about that, and I ignored it because—' She choked suddenly. He reached for her but she turned away quickly, throwing up her hands. 'Because I'm a fool.'

'No, because you love me, as I love you.'

'Oh, please!' she cried. Then her manner changed, became formal. 'Your Majesty can abandon those tactics now. They've served their purpose very nicely.'

'That's enough,' he shouted, seizing her shoulders and giving her a little shake. She tried to pull away but he tightened his hands. 'No, you're going to listen to me. I may not deserve it, but you're going to.'

She stood still in his hands, her eyes burning. 'Get it over with, then. It'll be a relief to us both to be done with this.'

'Everything you say was true about me in the beginning. I didn't treat you well. I mistrusted you, I deceived you, I lured you here and I had you burgled. I thought you were an adventuress and that was the only safe way to deal with you. I'm not proud of it, but I thought it was necessary.

'I was wrong. I came to realise that you weren't as I'd thought. I called my people in London and pulled them off the job.'

'Except that they'd already been through my house by then.'

'Unfortunately, yes. I did what I could. I was in love with you by that time. I tried to tell you about this the day you left, to prepare you. But I lost my nerve. I prayed that you'd never find out how I'd behaved, and that you and I could make a new and honest beginning.'

'But you planned to hide the truth about what you'd done. How honest is that?'

'Not very,' he admitted. 'But I was afraid. I couldn't face the thought of losing you.'

She didn't relent. 'The King is never afraid,' she said. 'You should remember that.'

'I'm afraid now,' he said quietly. 'More afraid than I've ever been in my life. At one time I couldn't have admitted to fear, but now I can. You did that for me. Now I see us drawing further apart and I don't know how to stop it.'

'There *is* no way to stop it,' she said wretchedly. 'And I don't want to.'

'Don't say that.' In an instant his fingers were over her lips, trying to silence the terrible words. But she shook herself free.

'It's too late,' she said fiercely. 'And you don't have to bother any more because I've got what you wanted. Here!' Near her on the floor stood a large canvas bag with two leather handles. She dumped it on the table between them and pulled it open to reveal the contents. Daniel stared at the mountain of papers within. 'There they are,' Lizzie said. 'Take them, and then we need never see each other again.'

'What—are these?'

'Alphonse's letters.'

'You had them all the time?'

'No. Only since yesterday. "Liz" gave them to me.'

'But she's been dead for years.'

'No. Dame Elizabeth has been dead for years, but she wasn't "Liz". We've all been barking up the wrong tree. It was Bess all the time.

'Her name is Elizabeth too, and people used to call her Liz for short. But Auntie ordered her to change it, because it was confusing to have a Liz and a Lizzie. So she became Bess, and of course I never knew her as anything else. But your grandfather did. She was always "Liz" to him. Look.'

She opened her purse and took out a picture. It was about ten years old, an amateurish family shot, showing the teenage Lizzie with the actress, standing haughtily, every inch the *grande dame*. Standing just behind them was a thin little woman with slightly untidy hair. Her dress was nondescript, her face was bare, its only adornment a cheerful smile. Daniel stared at her in disbelief.

'But she's—'

'Exactly,' Lizzie said. 'She's nothing to look at. Not beautiful or glamorous, not a titled lady or a star, not at all the sort of woman you'd expect to be a king's mistress. And she *was* his mistress. His letters leave no doubt of it.

'She was a servant, illegitimate, and in his world she'd have been called a nobody. But she has a great, generous spirit, and she was the love of his life.

'She's kept her secret all these years. But now she's dying, and when she had that attack she called me home so that she could give me these. She said I could do whatever I liked with them. So here they are. Take them, and forget I exist. You've got all you ever really wanted from me.'

In a daze Daniel began to draw the letters out, recognising his grandfather's handwriting even though there was something subtly different about it. It was larger, freer, and Alphonse, a man of few words, had covered endless sheets of paper, as though pouring out a soul.

Daniel went through one letter after another, glancing at each briefly, just long enough to still the last of his doubts.

'What did she say when she gave them to you?' he asked.

When there was no reply he looked up and found himself alone. Lizzie had gone.

Hurriedly he went out into the corridor, but it too was empty. A dreadful suspicion sent him to the window. She must have had a cab waiting all the time, he realised. All that could be seen of it now was the rear vanishing down the long avenue, until it reached the huge wrought-iron gates.

There was still time to stop her. All he had to do was call the gatekeeper. He reached for the telephone, but then checked himself. The habit of command was strong, but right now a command would lose him everything. Whatever he might say, she did not want to hear.

He stayed motionless, undecided, and as he watched the iron gates opened, the car went through, turned and vanished from sight.

CHAPTER SIX

IT WAS very quiet in the King's private rooms. The great clock in the corner silently proclaimed midnight, and the only sound was the rustling of paper on the big table that had been cleared of everything else. Outside the door Frederick sat with orders to permit nobody to disturb Daniel.

Nothing in his life had ever been so important as what he was doing now, fitting together the letters that had passed between two people for thirty years, until one of them had been cruelly struck down so that he could not even utter his beloved's name. It was more than a correspondence. It was a testimony of powerful, enduring love that awed him as he read.

Lizzie had said there was no doubt that they had been lovers in every sense of the word, and Daniel had already discerned as much from the 'Liz' letters. Yet they were relatively re-strained. Alphonse's were totally frank. He had loved this woman with his heart, his soul and his great, vigorous body. He had loved her fiercely, sexually, without false modesty or pride, and she had stimulated him to ignore his advancing years and love her with the urgent desire of a much younger man. Daniel, no prude, found himself blushing at some passages.

Yet this in itself was not the greatest surprise. That had come with the discovery that his grandfather, a strictly traditional man where 'a woman's place' was concerned, had turned to Liz for advice. As time passed she had become more than his lover. She had been his counsellor.

Suddenly Daniel grew still. His own name had leapt out at him from the paper.

I try to do my best by the boy, but what am I to do when he takes such wild ideas into his head? Why piano lessons? He's going to be a king, not join an orchestra.

Daniel read the phrase again and again, and suddenly time turned back and he was a boy of ten, wanting to learn the piano because it was only in making music that he could find the strength to cope with the pressures that were already threatening to crush him. But all authority had lain with his grandfather, who didn't understand, and who was impatient of explanation.

And then, out of the blue, Alphonse had yielded. A fine music master had been engaged and a new joy had entered Daniel's life. Yet even while he'd rejoiced he'd puzzled over his grandfather's *volte face*.

He went to the secret drawer where he'd kept the other side of the correspondence since Lizzie's first departure, yanking it out in a violent movement quite different from his usual restraint. The letters spilled all over the floor and he dropped to his knees, searching as though his life depended on it.

At last he found what he wanted: a letter from Liz in response.

Say yes to what he asks, my dearest. His life will be so hard. Indulge him and make his coming burden a

little easier. Let the poor child have some pleasure.
However much it is, it still won't be enough.

There was more. For years Alphonse had laid his personal
problems in his darling's hands and trusted her answers.
Daniel found the story of his childhood and teenage years
relived in these letters.

He remembered his father's death. How stiff and distant
Alphonse had seemed over the loss of his only son. It was
only to Liz that he had released the rage and pain that
consumed him. In letter after letter he'd let out a howl of
fatherly anguish.

Now he realised how much he'd overlooked when he'd
first glanced through these pages. The sight of his own name
in Liz's letters gave him a sensation that he'd never known
before, and which at first he couldn't identify. But it was a
good feeling—of being able to let down his guard in a trusted
presence. Where Alphonse had worried how he should rear
the future king, Liz had seen only the bereaved child.

He's just a little boy...let him be happy while he
can...make him safe...tell him you love him...don't let
him be ashamed to cry...be kind to him...be kind to
him...

Over weeks, months and years she had counselled love and
gentleness to the child.

In Daniel's mind those years were a blur. But now scenes
began to come back to him: himself at nine years old, fighting
back the tears even in the privacy of his own room, because
now he was heir to the throne, and a man, and men didn't cry.

Then his grandfather coming in, seeing the tears he was too late to hide. He'd waited to be blamed, but instead the stern face had softened, a kindly hand had rested on his shoulder, and a gruff voice had whispered, 'I know, my boy. I know.'

Other things. The music lessons—understood now for the first time. And Tiger, the mongrel, his own special care and his dearest friend. So much owed to this woman he'd never known.

Daniel took out the picture that Lizzie had left behind. It was hard to see much of Liz, standing in the shadows behind the other two. But he could make out the gentle glow of her face. And suddenly he could identify the unknown feeling that had eased his heart. His mother had died when he was a baby, and he'd never known a mother's love, but over the years and the miles Liz had tried to make up for that lack. And she'd succeeded more than any other woman could have done. Looking at her now, Daniel thought he could understand why.

He hadn't noticed the hours pass until Frederick knocked on the door. He answered it, but didn't allow him in. Frederick was startled at his pallor.

'Speak to my secretary,' Daniel commanded. 'Cancel any appointments I have for tomorrow. Say I'm detained on urgent business. And send me in some food.'

Through the night he worked, and then through the following day. When he came to an end he was unshaven and exhausted. But now he knew what he had to do.

She would sell the house, Lizzie decided as the plane headed back across the English channel. She had kept it almost as the Dame had left it, but now everything would remind her of the man who'd won her love with a lie. Just because she was a historian that didn't mean she must live in the past. With the house gone she would put everything behind her, abandon her book on Alphonse, and find a new life for herself.

Her anger lasted until she was indoors and under the shower. But the hot water couldn't lave her grief away and she let the tears come freely. She was a woman who never cried, but she cried now for the magic that had been a delusion, and for a feeling that she knew would never come again as long as she lived. Tonight she would let herself mourn what might have been. Tomorrow she would put it behind her and become a different woman, a more resolute and, if necessary, a harder one. Her mourning was for that too.

She spent the next day making plans. By evening the house bore a 'For Sale' notice and she told herself that things were proceeding wonderfully. Now all she wanted was to get out of here fast. She obtained some tea chests and began packing things away. With luck she could be out in a few days, leaving an agent to sell the house.

She worked blindly while the thoughts thrummed through her head. Everything that had happened in Voltavia had been an illusion, including Daniel's feelings. She'd been useful to him. Now he had what he wanted, and she was disposable. That was all there was to it. At least she had the advantage of knowing exactly where she stood. As she threw things into tea chests her anger mounted.

Midnight passed, then one, then two in the morning. With her mind in turmoil there was no point in going to bed. She was still working frantically when the front bell rang. She opened the door and at once a hand came through the gap, preventing her slamming it closed.

'Don't shut me out,' Daniel begged. 'Not until you've heard what I have to say.'

'We've said everything. Please go away Daniel. Nothing can make it right, and why bother?'

'Listen to me!' As she turned away he seized her shoulders fiercely. 'You have to.'

'Don't tell me what I have to do. I'm not one of your subjects.' She wrenched free and went into the kitchen to put on the kettle. It was a way of not looking at him. If he saw her face he might also see the leap of joy she hadn't been able to suppress at the sight of him. She thought she'd controlled it now, but she couldn't be sure, and it was wisest not to trust him.

He followed her and stood watching as she moved about. 'Not a word?' he asked at last. 'I turn up at this hour and you're not even curious?'

'What is there to be curious about? I'm sure you snapped your fingers and everybody jumped. Did they hold the plane for you?'

'There wasn't one. I chartered a special plane because all I could think of was getting to you. And I find a "For Sale" sign and you packing to leave.' His voice became tinged with anger. 'You really weren't going to give me a second chance, were you?'

'You don't need a second chance,' she cried. 'You've got everything you wanted. And you were brilliant. I'll give you that. You schemed and manipulated like a pro. But then, of course, you *are* a pro. A king would have to be. Well done, Your Majesty. But don't expect me to applaud and say it's all right.'

'Do you really believe that?' he asked quietly. 'You think there was nothing in my feelings for you but scheming?'

She shrugged. 'Why deny it? It's a perfectly honourable

position for a king. Not for a man, of course, but what does that matter? The man can always hide behind the king, and that's what you're good at.'

He was about to hurl an angry reply at her when he caught a look at her face and read in it the misery and exhaustion of the last thirty-six hours.

'I'll never forgive myself for hurting you,' he said. 'It's true I wasn't honest with you at the start, but I swear that was only for a short time. It didn't take me long to see how good and true you are, how much better than my fears. If you'll let me, I'll spend my life making it up to you.'

But his words washed over her. She couldn't answer. She could only look at him sadly, thinking of the chance that was lost for ever.

'How is Bess?' he asked.

'Holding on, but she's very weak. I'm visiting her today.'

'Good, because it's partly her that I came to see.'

'You can't be serious.'

'I was never more serious in my life. Since you left I've been reading all the letters—both sides of the correspondence, fitted together—and I've seen many things. I've seen that my grandfather wasn't at all the way he seemed, cold and remote. He was a man with a warm heart, which he found hard to show, except to her. But I've seen something else. Lizzie, you must let me meet Bess. I know now that she virtually raised me.'

'Whatever do you mean by that?'

'I mean that she guided my grandfather in his dealings with me. He'd have got everything wrong if she hadn't put him on the right path. I told you about the dog, the music lessons—it was her doing. But for her my life would have been so different, so much harder. She has been almost my mother, and I must thank her while there's still time.'

'She's a very old woman,' Lizzie said slowly. 'She hardly knows what's happening—'

'All the more reason for you to take me to her, today. And there's another reason—something I must tell her before anyone, even before you.'

His voice rang with sincerity but Lizzie was bruised from their last encounter. She searched his face, desperately seeking an answer.

'Lizzie, you must trust me,' he cried passionately. 'I beg you to believe me this one time.'

'Very well,' she said slowly. 'I'll take you to see Bess.'

Bess had come through her heart attack weak but lucid. They found her lying propped up against some pillows. She smiled at the sight of Lizzie, but her smile turned to awe when she saw Daniel. Frail though she was, she instinctively reached out a hand to him, and Daniel took it at once.

'You,' she whispered. 'You—'

Lizzie drew a quick, dismayed breath. 'Bess—it's not—'

'No, my dear, it's all right. I didn't really think—well, perhaps for a moment.'

To Lizzie's pleasure, Daniel sat beside the bed and spoke to Bess quite naturally. 'I believe I look very like my grandfather.'

'A little,' she conceded. Then her eyes twinkled as she added, 'Of course, he was *much* better looking. Just the same, I would have known you anywhere.'

'We have been acquainted for a long time,' Daniel said gently, 'although I've only just found out. It was you who softened his heart—'

'Oh, no,' Bess said quickly. 'He always had a great heart. But it was imprisoned. He used to say that I had set him free.'

'Yes,' Daniel said gravely. 'That's very easy for me to believe—now. Won't you please tell me about him. How did you meet?'

'It was fifty years ago. He came to London for the Queen's coronation, and he went to the theatre one evening. The show was *Dancing Time*, starring Lizzie Boothe. She wasn't Dame Elizabeth in those days, but she was at the height of her fame and beauty. After the performance he came backstage to meet the cast, and I was there too, lurking in the shadows to catch a glimpse of him. He noticed me and made someone bring me forward. My knees were knocking, I was so nervous. But he smiled at me, and suddenly I wasn't afraid any more.'

There was a hint of mischief in Bess's voice as she said, 'After that I was weak at the knees for another reason. He invited himself to lunch next day, and of course he brought an aide, and the aide whispered in my ear that His Majesty would like to speak to me alone. And when I saw him he told me that he loved me. It was as simple as that.'

'But what about the Dame?' Lizzie asked.

'She was our friend,' Bess said at once. 'She let us use her as "cover". It was all right for people to believe he admired her, in a theatrical kind of way. He once said, "I don't mind if people think I'm a glorified stage-door Johnny."'

'My grandfather *said* that?' Daniel asked, startled.

'Oh, yes. He had a very neat line in humour when he was in the mood.'

'I never saw him in that mood,' Daniel said regretfully.

'He kept it for me,' Bess sighed. 'And for the Dame, too, because he was grateful to her for helping us.'

'Didn't she mind?' Lizzie wanted to know.

'Only at first. She had so many conquests, and of course she'd have liked to add his scalp to her belt, for the fun of it. But when she saw how things stood she was very kind. And of course he gave her jewels and flowers, so the world *thought* she had his scalp, and that was really all she asked. She once told me that the situation suited her very well. "All the kudos and none of the inconvenience," was how she put it.'

'What did she mean, "inconvenience"?' Lizzie asked.

Bess paused before saying delicately, 'Well, my dear, contrary to appearances, the Dame wasn't a very *sensual* person. She liked to be admired from a distance. She used to say that frantic passion was all very well in its place, but it made such a mess of the hair. Alphonse was a very *vigorous* man, and I—well, let's just say that I never cared about my hair.'

'You're making me blush,' Daniel murmured.

'Well, it won't do you any harm,' Bess retorted with spirit. 'I wasn't always a dried-up old stick. And I have a very good memory.' She smiled, but she wasn't looking at them. 'Oh, yes, I remember everything. Everything he ever said to me—everything he did—every kiss—every whisper—'

Lizzie's eyes blurred, for suddenly the years had fallen away from Bess and she was once more the little maid, living in the shadows, in her thirties, thinking she would never know love. But then the most glorious man in the world had come striding into her life, caring nothing for the others but only for her and the special something she had to offer.

'He used to come over here incognito, whenever he could,' she said. 'Once we stole away and went to a fair. Nobody recognised him, and we went around all the stalls. He won this at the coconut shy, and gave it to me.' She pointed to the cheap ring on her finger. 'It was the only jewel I'd let him give me. He wanted to give me some of his family jewels. I couldn't let him, of course—the scandal—so he made a financial settlement on me, so that I should never be in want.'

'So that's how you could afford this place,' Lizzie said.

'That's right. Oh, if you could have seen his face when he told me about the money! He was so afraid that I'd be offended. Money might have meant that I was a certain kind of woman, you see.'

'But a man expects to provide for his wife,' Daniel said. 'And in his heart you were his wife and Queen.'

'That's what he said. We used to talk of the day when I could come to Voltavia and live in a little cottage near him. But it was all a pipe dream. People would have known and looked down on me and, although I wouldn't have minded, he would have minded for me. And besides, I couldn't leave the Dame. She'd been good to me, and she was getting old and blind. He understood that my duty had to come first. He said it made him love me more.

'I used to think that when she no longer needed me I might go out to him at last, and hang what people said. But then he had a stroke. They said it was savage and terrible, cutting him down in a moment, and all communication between us was cut off, so cruelly. He couldn't write to me, and I didn't dare write to him. It was as though he was dead. And yet I knew he was alive, longing for me.'

'He always knew that you loved him,' Daniel said. 'I didn't know anything of this at the time, but I'm certain of this.'

Bess smiled. 'How like him you are. Now I can see it. You have his eyes and his loving heart.' She laid a feeble hand on

Lizzie's. 'You're very lucky my dear. When the men of this family love, they really know how to love. It's very exciting.'

Lizzie's eyes met Daniel's. 'Yes, it is,' she murmured.

Daniel took Bess's hands between both his, and spoke very gently. 'I had a special reason for coming to see you. I have a letter—his last letter—one that you never received.'

'I don't understand.'

'He must have been in the middle of writing it and laid it aside because he wasn't feeling well, and the stroke caught him before he could take it up again... At all events, it was found locked away with your letters to him. He never had the chance to finish it, and so you never received it.'

Lizzie stared at him. 'I had no idea...'

'It was the surprise I had for you before you left,' he told her. 'That was how much I'd come to trust you by then, but things went wrong for us.' He took out a sheet of paper and carefully placed it in Bess's hand. 'After all these years, this is his last message to you.'

The old woman's voice was husky. 'I can't see—read it for me, please—'

Daniel moved very close to her and took one of her hands in his.

'"My dearest love,"' he read, '"always dearer to me than anyone else on earth, because you know everything about me, and love me in spite of the worst—my heart is heavy tonight because yesterday we parted. Perhaps it is only for a little while, and we may still hope for the next meeting, in a month, as we discussed. But as I grow older I fear that each parting may be the last, and I may never again have the chance to tell you what you are, and have been to me.

'"And so I set it down, in the hope that when I can no

longer say the words it will somehow reach you. Others see you occupying a lowly position, but to me you will always be a great, great lady: the woman who brought my heart to life and showed me what love could be. I lived encased in stone until you broke me free."'

'You sound—just like him,' Bess murmured.

'I was just like him,' Daniel said softly. 'Until my Lizzie came to me. Encased in stone, needing to be set free. But only if she wishes.'

Bess regarded Lizzie with eyes that saw everything. 'Whatever he has done to offend you,' she said shrewdly, 'it is as nothing beside the love that you share. Throw the defences away, my dear. They have no place about your heart.'

'Yes,' Lizzie said with her eyes on Daniel. 'I know that.'

'Finish the letter for me,' Bess pleaded.

'There isn't very much more,' Daniel said, taking up the page again. '"*I do not know what the future holds,*"' he read. '"*But I am certain that it must be a future together. If not in this world, then in another that we cannot even imagine. However long the wait, I shall watch for you with my arms open and my heart as much yours as on the day—*"' He stopped. 'That's where it finishes.'

'It is enough.' Tears were streaming from Bess's eyes. 'He always promised not to leave me without a last message, and he was a man of his word. Oh, my dears, my dears—if only you could be as happy as I am—'

Two hours later Bess slipped quietly out of life. Daniel and Lizzie were with her as she fell asleep, still holding her beloved's final letter. When they had both kissed her Lizzie took the paper gently from Bess's fingers.

'I'll put it back before the funeral,' she said. 'And it can be buried with her.'

'Would you like to have her taken to Voltavia and placed near him?'

After a moment's hesitation Lizzie shook her head. 'Thank you, but there's no need. I believe that they're together now, and that's what matters.'

'And what becomes of us?'

'What do you want to become of us, my love?'

'Be my wife, and keep me always in your heart, for only there will I be safe.'

Six weeks later King Daniel of Voltavia married Elizabeth Boothe in a small private ceremony, attended only by his children and a few trusted friends. His daughter was a bridesmaid, and his sons, following royal convention, shared the role of groom's supporters.

There was much talk about the King's wedding gift to his bride: a fabulous diamond set, including a tiara, necklace, bracelets and earrings. But nobody knew of his real gift to her: the complete correspondence between King Alphonse and 'Liz', with his permission to publish it as she pleased.

Nor did anybody know that she had thanked him and refused to publish—the first time in Voltavia's history that the King's bride had turned down his wedding gift and made her husband a happy man by doing so.

But Lizzie had one final gift for the man she loved and who loved her beyond anything he could express in words. On their wedding night they stood before the great open fire in his apartment and tossed the letters—every last one—into the flames, watching until there was nothing left.

He took her into his arms. 'No regrets at depriving history?'

'No regrets,' she assured him lovingly. 'We've done them justice. History would never have understood them as we do, and only the future matters now.'